THE
STUPENDOUS
SONNY

THE STUPENDOUS SONNY

ELLIE CLEMENTS

BLOOMSBURY
CHILDREN'S BOOKS
LONDON OXFORD NEW YORK NEW DELHI SYDNEY

BLOOMSBURY CHILDREN'S BOOKS
Bloomsbury Publishing Plc
50 Bedford Square, London WC1B 3DP, UK
29 Earlsfort Terrace, Dublin 2, Ireland

BLOOMSBURY, BLOOMSBURY CHILDREN'S BOOKS and the Diana
logo are trademarks of Bloomsbury Publishing Plc

First published in Great Britain in 2023 by Bloomsbury Publishing Plc

Text copyright © Ellie Clements, 2023
Illustrations copyright © Chaaya Prabhat, 2023

A catalogue record for this book is available from the British Library

ISBN: PB: 978-1-5266-3837-3; eBook: 978-1-5266-3836-6;
ePDF: 978-1-5266-3835-9

2 4 6 8 10 9 7 5 3 1

Typeset by RefineCatch Limited, Bungay, Suffolk

Printed and bound in Great Britain by CPI Group (UK) Ltd,
Croydon CR0 4YY

To find out more about our authors and books visit www.bloomsbury.com
and sign up for our newsletters

For Dylan

CHAPTER 1

Have you ever had a dream that felt so remarkable and so real, that you woke up wondering if it really was a dream?

Well, I have!

I've had this type of dream three times now, except each dream was a little bit different from the other. The first dream was two weeks ago, the night of my twelfth birthday party. In the dream, I was lying flat on my bed when suddenly I began to float upwards. I felt completely weightless, just as I imagine it would feel to be an astronaut on the moon. I must have reached about a metre above my bed before I woke up.

I'd never had a dream like that before, yet there was something about it which made the dream feel like it had really happened. Of course, it couldn't have, because people can't levitate, right?

I wondered if my VERY REALISTIC LEVITATING dream was caused by all the cheese sandwiches I'd eaten at my birthday party. After all, cheese is supposed to give you NIGHTMARES. Not that my dream was a nightmare. It was *splendtaculous*, which a word I made up, only because there are no words in the dictionary that are incredible enough to describe what levitating had felt like. And anyway, the cheese I'd eaten was made out of coconuts and not dairy, which I'm allergic to.

So then I started wondering if my dream was all down to how miserable I'd been feeling after my mum had to leave my party early to catch a flight to Jordan. She's a movie make-up artist and she was off to join the shoot of the sequel to my favourite film ever, *A Mission to Mars*. It's such a cool job because she gets to make actors and actresses in films look like were-wolves, zombies, aliens, you name it, plus she gets to work in different places all over the world! But this means she spends a lot of time away from home, which to me is the uncool part of Mum's job because I always miss her loads. I wasn't going to be seeing her for three whole months! So I suppose you could say I had flying on my mind, because I did think how great it would've been to have flown off with Mum, just to avoid another sad goodbye. And of course, I would've got a nice, sunny holiday too!

So that had to be the explanation for my dream. Right?

CHAPTER 2

My second VERY REALISTIC LEVITATING dream happened six nights ago. Once again it was the middle of the night and I felt wide awake, and this time I was higher in the air, my face practically touching the ceiling.

As I shifted upright, I discovered I was able to move, and went over to my wardrobe. All the while my heart was drumming in my chest because I was … FLYING! And even though I was shocked by it all, I felt elated because it was so amazing.

And there's more, because not only was I flying but so was half the contents of my room!

My jacket that was hung on the back of my door suddenly sprang off the hook, and it was as if an invisible person were wearing it as it swung and swayed through the air, while the blanket that had been on my bed was flying about like a magic carpet. Some of my books and comics had come whizzing off the shelves, their pages flapping like wings, and a pair of socks I'd left on the floor raced round the room, one chasing the other as if they were playing a game of It. I had an old space rocket orbiting around me, and a small globe that had been on my desk was spinning on its axis in mid-air. And the rubbish in my waste-paper bin was floating up like sky lanterns. I can't tell you how fantastic it all was, but it was a little stressful too, if I'm being honest. I also had this weird buzzing sound in my head.

Was it me making everything move? I thought.

I called out to my dad because he needed to see this. Suddenly something struck my head. I think it was one of my flying books, or it might've been my toy rocket. The next thing I knew, I was back in my bed, Dad gently shaking me awake.

'Looks like you were having a bad dream, kiddo, but I'm here now,' he whispered.

I sat up, looking around my room, which was no different from how it usually looked and there was certainly nothing flying about. My jacket was on the back of the door, my books were on the bookshelves, and my globe and space rocket were on my desk.

Now you're probably thinking that I *had* to have been dreaming, but it had all felt very, very real.

'You were calling me in your sleep. What were you dreaming about?' asked Dad.

'I was … flying,' I murmured slowly.

'That doesn't sound like too bad a dream. I happen to think flying dreams are the best type of dreams a person can have!' said Dad. 'They're certainly better than those dreams where all your teeth fall out,' he mumbled, rolling his lips in to do an impression of someone with no teeth, which made me giggle.

My dad is very good at doing impressions and accents. He's an actor, so he can do them easy-peasy. I like his animal impressions the best, particularly his horse and bald eagle.

'Would you like me to stay with you for a bit or do you think you'll be OK?' he asked.

'I'll be OK.'

Dad nodded. 'Well, try and get some sleep,' he said, switching off my lamp. 'Night, night, Stupendous Sonny,' he whispered.

That was my mum and dad's nickname for me – Stupendous Sonny. They've called me that ever since I was a baby because on the night I was born, my parents saw a shooting star which they reckoned meant I was a pretty special kid, one meant for greatness.

As soon as Dad wandered out, I switched my lamp back on and stayed awake, my eyes scanning the room, waiting for a book to launch up into the air or something else. But my eyes must have started to close, and I was fast asleep again.

CHAPTER 3

My most recent VERY REALISTIC LEVITATING dream was just last night, and it was even more extraordinary than the first two. This time, I was levitating above my bed again, and there was this tingly feeling in my arms and legs which was even more random. Next thing I knew, I was standing in the garden. I was shivering, because it was quite chilly and I was in my PJs. The grass was tickling the soles of my feet, and as I walked towards the house to get back inside, my arms and legs began to tingle again, and a second later I was in the kitchen. Only I hadn't gone through the back door, so I don't know how I managed to get there so fast, and bizarrely, I was holding a tub of butter. But before I had the chance to figure out what was happening, my body started tingling again and I was in the bathroom, sitting in the bath. I got another tingly feeling, then a split second later I was waking up in my bed. When I checked the time on my alarm clock it was 2.34 a.m.

I told myself it was just another dream and tried to get back to sleep. But here's the crazy thing which brings me to today: when I woke up this morning at 7 a.m., the same time I normally wake up, and looked at my feet, they were dirty. And trust me, they didn't look like that before I went to bed. So it left me wondering if my dream was actually something else entirely. Something amazing, something *astrobulous*! Which is a word I made up to mean something better than anything in the whole galaxy!

Was it possible that I, Sonny Lawson of 22 Eden Avenue, Delmere, the most boring town on earth, had … SUPERPOWERS?! And I should know all about super-powers, considering I'm a big fan of superhero films and comics.

I'm guessing this probably sounds impossible, and I honestly wouldn't blame you for thinking that, seeing as I'm just your ordinary, average kind of kid. In fact, I'm so ordinary and average that if there were ever an award for the Most Ordinary and Average Kid in the World, I'm sure I'd stand a good chance of winning. So even though my nickname is Stupendous Sonny, there's very little I'm stupendous at. I've never won a competition, unlike my ten-year-old sister Ramona, who's won several writing and magazine competitions. And I can't even beat my brother Oscar, who's seven, at my favourite video game, *Star Stacks*. So far, he's collected 52,000 stars while I've only collected 38,000.

I'm pretty average in most of my subjects at school, unlike my best friend Elliot Wilkins, who's a proper brainbox. I'm not popular, nor am I good at sports, even though I'm in my school's athletics team – more on that later. And there really isn't much that's interesting about me, not even my name. I'm named after no one, whereas Ramona's named after our granny (our dad's mum) and Oscar's named after the coveted award that my mum hopes to win one day. Plus, there's nothing that would make me stand out from a crowd, not even the lightning bolts shaved into my hair.

So believe me, I'm the last person you'd ever think would unexpectedly and extraordinarily gain super-powers!

I realised I was going to need some help in working out if my dreams really were superpowers, and luckily there was someone I knew who'd be up for solving my BIG DREAM MYSTERY – my best friend Elliot.

CHAPTER 4

'The dreams have been different but at the same time similar. They're probably what you'd call a recurring dream,' I said to Elliot as I was explaining it all to him during break at school.

'But you can't work out if the dreams were real or not, is that what you're saying?'

I nodded.

'So you reckon you can fly and, by the sounds of it, teleport?' said Elliot.

His face looked completely disbelieving, which made me realise how ridiculous I must've sounded.

Still, Elliot was intrigued by what I had to say, and we continued the conversation during lunch.

'I also think I must've moved the tub of butter with

my mind, because what other way is there to explain it being on the kitchen table this morning?'

I remembered putting the butter on the table just before I somehow ended up in the bathtub. The butter is always kept in the fridge and Dad was quick to notice.

'Who left this butter here?' he had asked when we all came down for breakfast.

'Not me,' said Ramona, taking a box of Rice Krispies out of the cupboard.

'Or me,' said Oscar, and when Dad looked at me for an answer, I could only shrug.

'How many times have I told all of you about leaving stuff out that belongs in the fridge?' he responded with a sigh.

Elliot thought about what I said. 'Did you make yourself some toast before you went to bed? Because maybe you just forgot that you left the butter out.'

'No, I didn't have any toast! Plus, that butter wasn't even the one I eat. My butter is dairy-free and that one *was* in the fridge.'

'You're not making this up, are you?' said Elliot, his face looking cynical.

I shook my head at him. 'I can't believe you'd think I'd make something like this up. How long have we been friends?'

'Since the Ice Age, I know,' he replied, blowing out his cheeks.

That was something me and Elliot liked to say, seeing as we've known each other for longer than we can even remember. We first met at playgroup when we were two years old.

'Well, it's certainly a mystery,' said Elliot, stroking his chin. 'But you have to know, Sonny, that it's just not scientifically possible for people to have superpowers. So I really don't think that's what's behind your BIG DREAM MYSTERY.'

'They don't feel like dreams though,' I persisted. 'And why did my feet have mud on them this morning if—'

'I've got it!' Elliot interrupted. 'I think I know what's going on.'

'What?'

'I think you might've been sleepwalking.'

'Hmm,' I murmured, considering this. 'But that still doesn't explain the dream where stuff was moving around my bedroom, and I was able to fly.'

'I still think you dreamed that. But when you found yourself in the garden and bathroom, I reckon that was you sleepwalking.'

'DO YOU SLEEPWALK?' a voice suddenly boomed behind us.

13

It was a boy in our form called Parvin Singh, who was with another boy called Zeki Osman.

Parvin's my arch-nemesis and we've been enemies since primary school. So the last thing I wanted was for him to tell the whole cafeteria that I sleepwalk. And thanks to Parvin, kids started looking at me and giggling.

'I don't sleepwalk!' I retorted.

'So why did I just hear Elliot say you do?' said Parvin.

'We were speaking hypothetically, if you even know what that means.' Elliot sprang to my defence.

'I do, yeah,' Parvin replied, but with an unsure expression.

'Anyway, didn't your parents ever tell you that you shouldn't go around eavesdropping on other people's conversations?' said Elliot.

'No,' said Parvin bluntly. There was an awkward silence for a moment. 'So is there any chance of you guys getting over the high jump bar today?' Parvin said, then burst out laughing, along with Zeki.

I did say I'd tell you more about how I came to be in my school's athletics team, and this is despite being rubbish at the high jump, which is my sport. Elliot does the high jump too, but he's not much better. Parvin and Zeki are both runners – Parvin the 400m, and Zeki the 200m – and unlike me and Elliot, they're really good.

'Yeah, the way you fell on to the bar last week had me cracking up for days!' said Zeki to me. 'But I guess you must be used to it now, seeing as you can't jump to save your life!'

'How on earth did you ever get on the team?' said Parvin as he and Zeki shook their heads.

They well and truly knew how I did. Mr Jarvis, head of PE and our school's athletics coach, had desperately been looking for some high jumpers. Hardly any kids took part in the trials except me, Elliot and a boy called Liam Sidwell, who was even more hopeless than we were. Still, I was pleased that I made it on to the team, especially after my unsuccessful try-outs for the boys' football and basketball teams.

But despite all the effort and practice Elliot and I put in, neither of us has ever cleared 1.30m, our goal height.

'I think you *are* a sleepwalker,' said Parvin, then paused for a second in readiness for the punchline, a smile creeping across his face. 'You've been sleepwalking into the high jump bar ever since you joined the athletics team!'

'Oh, you're so funny. NOT!' I said as Parvin grinned with glee, a grin I annoyingly saw again during our after-school practice session when I failed to clear 1.26m for the fifth time that afternoon.

15

As I'd strode towards the bar to take my jump, I'd extended my upper body too early.

CLANK!!!

For what felt like the millionth time, the bar came down.

'Aw, what a shame,' said Parvin as he and Zeki gave me a patronising applause. 'When will you realise, Sonny, that you're just not meant for greatness like myself?'

'Oh shut up!' I replied but it was *so* humiliating.

Now, I'm not one for showing off, but I would've loved to have blurted out to them that I probably have superpowers. It would've been so good to have had the last laugh, even though I know that, just like Elliot, they wouldn't have believed me.

But I came to a decision that there was in fact no BIG DREAM MYSTERY and that I truly did have super-powers. And as far as I was concerned, neither Elliot nor anyone else was going to change my mind.

CHAPTER 5

I was certain my brother Oscar would believe I had superpowers, so I couldn't wait to tell him when I got home after high jump practice. As soon as I stepped into the house, I was greeted by a familiar but irritating smell. It was Mrs Armstrong's chicken stew. She's our next-door neighbour who often babysits us. I had hoped, now that I was twelve, I wouldn't need any more babysitting, but annoyingly my mum and dad thought differently.

It was so unfair because it's not as if I'm a little kid like Ramona and Oscar. I'm almost a teenager! Plus, I was sick of eating chicken stew! It was Mrs Armstrong's speciality dish but was literally the only thing she ever cooked.

'The stew is just heating up, so dinner will be ready soon,' she said when I went into the living room, where she, Ramona and Oscar were. She was watching the news, which was basically all she ever watched.

I tried my best to look enthusiastic that we were having chicken stew yet again, though honestly, a plate of cold baked beans would've been more exciting. Not that I expect Mrs Armstrong to make us that for dinner any time soon. In her opinion, no other meal comes close to being as tasty and as healthy as her stew. But there's only so much stew a boy can eat, and trust me, I've had more than my fair share.

Ramona was busy doing her homework on the carpet while Oscar was watching his favourite cartoon series, *The Power Piglets*, on the family iPad. I pretended to snatch the iPad as I said hello, and he turned round and thumped me on the arm.

'Oscar!' Mrs Armstrong scowled. 'What are you doing punching Sonny?!'

'He was trying to take the iPad from me!' Oscar bleated.

'I was only joking, Osc,' I said, rubbing my arm.

I should've known not to come between Oscar and *The Power Piglets*. They're a group of superpowered piglets that can fly and shoot lasers out of their eyes. Oscar has the full set of fluffy toys, as well as sticker books, a Power Piglets lunch box, a Power Piglets duvet set and a Power Piglets lamp that projects colourful flying piglets on to the walls. He also has a pair of Power Piglets pyjamas that he reckons gives him powers of his own – the ability to stay awake beyond eight o'clock.

'They give you the power to be cheeky,' I've heard Mrs Armstrong say to him more than once.

Even though Oscar's a little kid, he felt like the right person to talk to about my superpowers, and unlike Elliot, I was sure he'd be much more excited for me and wouldn't try to convince me that I'd been sleepwalking.

'Hey, Osc, do you want to hear a secret?' I whispered, leaning over the sofa.

'What secret?' he said, without looking up from the iPad.

'It's about superpowers like what the Power Piglets have.'

He turned round again.

'I know someone with superpowers,' I whispered, then beckoned him out to the hall.

'Who do you know with superpowers?' he asked impatiently.

'Me!'

Oscar threw me a mocking look.

'You don't have superpowers!' he snorted.

'I do, Oscar, seriously. Like the Power Piglets. I can fly.'

Oscar crossed his arms. 'Show me then. Fly now.'

'Erm, it doesn't quite work like that. It only happens at night, for some reason, and before you say anything,

I wasn't dreaming it! I did think that at first, but I just know my powers are real.'

'I don't believe you,' said Oscar.

'You don't?' I whispered, feeling crushed.

I thought Oscar of all people would've believed me, considering he believes in the Tooth Fairy, Father Christmas and the Easter Bunny. He flat out refuses to believe it's so obviously our parents putting money under his pillow or presents under the tree or a chocolate Easter egg at the foot of his bed. Even when my parents confessed to being the Tooth Fairy when Oscar's money demands became way too steep (he was threatening to write a very angry letter to the Tooth Fairy because they were leaving his friend Dominic three pounds per tooth while he was only getting one pound), Oscar still wouldn't accept that the Tooth Fairy wasn't real.

'What are you two whispering about?' said Ramona, coming out into the hall.

'Sonny's trying to make out he has superpowers,' said Oscar, which made Ramona laugh snidely.

'You're such a donut,' she said, rolling her eyes at me.

'It's true, I do have powers!' I insisted, despite knowing I stood no chance of convincing Ramona.

If only there was a way I could make my superpowers appear at a time that wasn't the dead of the night, then they'd believe me.

CHAPTER 6

Trying to get my superpowers to appear again was feeling harder than the high jump. Over the next few days, I can't tell you the number of times I stared at a pencil or a book, trying to make them move with my mind. And jumping off my bed one morning in the hope I'd soar up to the ceiling only led to Dad having a go at me after I came crashing down to the floor with a thud.

'SQUASHED TOMATOES! What on earth was that noise?!' he said, marching into my room. 'You sounded like you were about to come through the ceiling!' he added dramatically. Well, he is an actor.

'I was just doing some exercises,' I told him quickly.

'But why do you have to make such a racket?' he asked, and shook his head.

It was so annoying the way Dad was making such a fuss. I mean, he never fusses when Oscar is singing *The Power Piglets'* theme tune at the top of his voice or when Ramona's moaning about something – which is why I have this nickname for her: Moaner.

My twelfth birthday party was almost ruined because of all the moaning she was doing, all because she wasn't happy there was no sweet chilli sauce to go with the duck spring rolls Mum had made. I was fine to have them with tomato ketchup, seeing as I absolutely love ketchup, but Ramona just kept going on and on, and she wouldn't stop complaining about all the sandwiches being coconut cheese. She wanted Dad to make her some stinky egg mayo sandwiches instead and had a big pout on her face when Dad said there wasn't time. I mean, we were already an hour into my party, and I was just about to blow out the candles on my cake.

You'd think my parents would've been cross with my sister for all the moaning she was doing. Except it was me they were cross with. It was *me* who got into trouble at my own birthday party for simply asking Moaner to STOP moaning!

'Sonny! Will you not call your sister that name?!' said Dad. 'You know it's not nice. Now, tell her you're sorry.'

'But why should I? It's my party and she's trying to

spoil it!' I protested, feeling properly miffed at how Dad was embarrassing me in front of my guests.

'Well, you just won't get any cake,' he said, picking up my birthday cake from the table as I looked at him in astonishment.

He was genuinely threatening to take away my birthday cake when I still hadn't even blown out the candles!

Naturally, I couldn't let him do that, and besides, it was a chocolate cake and I love chocolate, especially the dairy-free kind.

'All right,' I huffed, and turned to my sister, who was looking ever so smug. '*Sorry*,' I muttered.

Sometimes it feels like my parents reserve all their tellings-off just for me. They'll usually say it's because I'm the eldest and I 'should know better', like the time I got blamed for breaking a vase when it was Oscar who'd wanted to play football in the house. OK, I admit I *did* kick the ball into the vase, but the only reason why I agreed to play the game was that Oscar kept saying how bored he was. So I was doing him a favour! Yet it was me who got into trouble while Oscar got off scot-free.

Back to my superpowers, or lack of, because they weren't even appearing at night, let alone during the day. It was like my powers had disappeared altogether. When

I told Elliot this, he just saw it as proof that I never had them in the first place.

'Superpowers aren't real, Sonny. That's just a fact you're going to have to accept,' he said.

But no way was I willing to accept that.

CHAPTER 7

A few more days later, my superpowers finally returned, and this time they appeared most unexpectedly. Even more excitingly, they appeared during the day!

So, to give you a rundown of events leading up to a moment that I can only describe as *ginomenal*, which is a word that's even more special than *astrobulous*, I'd just arrived at school with Elliot, having met up with him at the bus stop round the corner. I usually walk to the bus stop as I don't live that far from school, but Elliot has to get the bus in every day. There are two main entrances to our school, Sandall Rise: the east, which is the quickest way to get to our form class, and the west, which is the long way round.

Normally we avoid the east entrance, because it's where a boy called Milo Allerton and his gang are on unofficial sentry duty every morning. Milo is the scariest boy at Sandall Rise who HATES Year Sevens like me, which is why he and his gang have banned Year Sevens from going that way. And if any of us even dare to step on the path, then we can expect a vicious shelling of chewing-gum missiles.

A girl in my form called Holly once got a chewing-gum missile stuck in her hair. She had to get the gum cut out, which meant she had to get a new haircut, which she was very upset about. I don't have much hair for a chewing-gum missile to stick to, but I still wouldn't want to be chased by Milo, considering he's a Year Nine who looks more like a Year Twelve! Milo allegedly has a whole arsenal of these missiles, and they say he chews up to thirty sticks of gum a day (which can't be very good for your teeth, might I add), just so he's got them to hand should a brave Year Seven take their chances.

According to Elliot, his bus had been stuck in extra-slow traffic this morning, so had the two of us taken the west entrance, we definitely would've been late and received a deathly stare from our form teacher Mr Solomons. It's a stare that would even have Darth Vader quaking in his boots. Mr Solomons just hates it when kids are late to registration. Elliot and I knew that if we were going to be on time, we had to take the east entrance. So we came up with a quick strategy of how we'd survive a missile attack.

'We'll protect ourselves with our rucksacks and just run as fast as we can,' said Elliot, and it did sound like a strategy that would work. Plus, it was very simple, and wouldn't involve us having to beg for mercy like the time Liam became a target and had chewing gum raining down on him.

Normally Milo was very alert, like he could smell when a Year Seven was about to try to run past him, but today he was distracted by his friend Omar, who was talking animatedly about something, giving Elliot and me the perfect opportunity to seize the moment. So after giving each other the nod, our rucksacks held in front of us like shields, we made a dash for it. Straight away Milo and his gang were chasing us.

'OI! YOU TWO ARE DEAD MEAT!' Milo was shouting.

As they gained on us, Elliot and I got split up, which certainly wasn't part of the strategy.

THWACK!!!

As I entered the school building, a missile hit the back of my neck. Kids were rushing to their classrooms, but I just knew Milo was still behind me. I wasn't quite sure where to run or hide, but I took my chances on the first door I came to – the caretaker's storeroom. It smelt very strongly of detergent, which tickled my nostrils. I was going to sneeze, and Milo was standing right outside.

'Where did that Year Seven go?' I heard him say, my heart thump-thump-thumping.

'Dunno, but he's got to be around here somewhere,' I heard his friend Charlie say.

Meanwhile my nostrils were tickling more and more. I tried wriggling them around to hold in the sneeze.

'Just wait until I find that kid,' Milo grunted. 'I'm gonna smash his face in!'

'ATCHOO!!!' All at once, a giant sneeze burst from me. It sounded so loud that I wouldn't have been surprised if astronauts in space heard it.

'Someone's in there!' a voice said.

My heart pounded harder, despite the voice not sounding like Milo's. It sounded like Mr Pearson, the caretaker.

'Whoever's in there, you've got five seconds to come out … or else!'

I wasn't sure I wanted to know what the 'else' was that he was referring to, especially if it meant getting a huge telling-off from Mrs Somerville, the head teacher, or having to spend a whole week in detention.

But it was all too late – the doorknob began to turn, and as I reluctantly took a step forward, knowing I'd just have to accept my fate, suddenly my body began to tingle and I was no longer there!

Instead I was standing in the middle of a tennis court with another missile heading my way. Only this one wasn't chewing gum … It was a very fast tennis ball!

CHAPTER 8

CLONK!!!

I'm not sure how I managed to duck so rapidly, because the tennis ball must have been coming towards me at ninety miles per hour at least. But I was completely shocked to even be on the tennis court, and so were the two men who'd been playing.

'Where did you spring from?' said one of them, striding towards me.

'It's like he came out of nowhere, Bill!' said the other man. 'And shouldn't you be in school, kid?' he added.

I didn't say anything and instead ran off.

Thankfully I knew where I was – Fern Park – but it was at least a fifteen-minute walk away from school. I was definitely going to miss registration now, which

I suppose on the plus side meant I'd avoid Mr Solomons's deathly stare. I'd most likely get a 'What time do you call this?' from Mrs Banerjee, my geography teacher. Not that she'd believe me if I told her that after hiding in Mr Pearson's storeroom to escape a brutal shelling of chewing-gum missiles and sneezing so loud to wake a bear out of hibernation, I had somehow managed to teleport myself to the park right in the middle of someone's tennis game. Yeah, as if she'd believe that!

As I sprinted in the direction of school, I felt happy that my superpowers were back! Only, I couldn't work out why and how I'd teleported myself to Fern Park. I suppose my life had flashed before my eyes right before I teleported as I was scared of what would happen if Milo or Mr Pearson caught me. I thought of my mum, my dad, Ramona, Oscar, our house, our street, playing video games, studying the stars through my telescope, eating ice cream in my favourite ice-cream parlour, and I guess a thought about Fern Park must've been amongst all of that.

'CAREFUL!' said a woman, whom I ran straight into. I was so keen to get back to school that I hadn't been paying much attention to my surroundings.

I was outside a building called The Archer, which is a health club. My mum, however, reckons it's the base of a shadowy secret society, even though my dad, who once considered joining, confirmed that it was a health club which supposedly had a swimming pool that was much nicer than the public pool we go to.

But there was something about the building that always gave me the shivers. You couldn't see inside because of its reflective windows, and on the roof was a statue of a scary-faced goblin holding a bow and arrow. So I happen to agree with Mum that The Archer is the headquarters of a secret society. But unlike her, I think its members and staff are shapeshifting aliens hell-bent on taking over the world, just like the Skrulls in my favourite comic, *Secret Invasion*.

'I'm sorry,' I said to the woman as I tried to catch my breath.

'Just look where you're going, in future,' she replied sternly.

When I finally made it back to school, I took the west entrance, even though Milo would've been in a lesson. I still didn't want to take any chances.

'I didn't realise you were in today,' said Mrs Banerjee, as I walked into the classroom and sat down next to Elliot.

'Sorry, miss, my alarm clock forgot to go off this morning,' I fibbed, which made a few kids giggle.

She raised an eyebrow, but that was it.

'So what happened? Did Milo catch up with you?' whispered Elliot, as Mrs Banerjee continued drawing a volcano on the board with fiery molten lava spurting out of it.

'No, I hid. What about you?'

'His friend Aiden chased me for a bit, but I managed to lose him. I was worried when I didn't see you at registration. I thought Milo had got you. So where did you hide?'

'In Mr Pearson's storeroom. But the real reason why I'm so late is because –' I leaned in to whisper straight into Elliot's ear – '*I teleported to Fern Park.*'

'You did what?' said Elliot loudly, making Mrs Banerjee turn round.

'Do you have a question, Elliot?' she asked, her eyebrows rising once again.

'No, I don't, miss,' he replied quickly.

'Perhaps you'd like to describe to the class what triggers a volcanic eruption?' she said.

'Erm … er …'

'Maybe if you'd been paying attention, you'd know,' she responded, with a face that wasn't best pleased.

'I'll tell you about it later,' I whispered to Elliot.

I didn't want to get him into any more trouble.

'So somehow you found yourself in the middle of someone's tennis game?' said Elliot, as I explained more during break. 'And are you sure you didn't sleepwalk there?'

'Oh, come on, Elliot, surely you don't think I fell asleep in Mr Pearson's storeroom and sleepwalked *all* the way to Fern Park from school, through traffic, past strangers and everything else?'

'But nobody has superpowers, Sonny.'

'I do! Why can't you just believe me?'

'Because it's not humanly possible for people to teleport or move things with their mind or do anything else that's beyond explanation.'

'All right. Well, I'll prove to you right now that I can do those things.'

I tried to think of a discreet way I could prove to him that I had superpowers.

'So, you're going to teleport right here in the play-ground, are you?' said Elliot, looking at me cynically.

'I'd rather not have an audience so I'll, erm ...' I reached into my rucksack and took out my house keys. 'I'll see if I can move my keys with my mind.'

I put the keys on the bench where we were sitting, but I gave up before I'd even started.

'I still don't know how to make my powers work because they just happen randomly,' I said in a weary voice. 'So I have no idea how to get these keys to move. Ugh! It's so annoying!'

'I reckon you've been daydreaming as well as night-dreaming your powers,' Elliot replied.

'I'm telling you, they're not dreams, and today I was definitely wide awake!'

I was starting to feel like I was going round and round in circles. Why did no one believe me?!

Just then a hand snatched up my keys.

'Thanks for these, Sonny!' said Parvin, jangling them in the air.

I leaped up. 'Give them back!' I said, trying to grab them.

'You're gonna have to jump much higher than that,' said Parvin, as he held my keys high above his head while Zeki stood next to him, laughing hysterically. 'You might even have to beat your personal best. But we all know your personal best is pretty lousy, so it looks like I'll be keeping these keys!'

It didn't help that Parvin was much taller than me, and he kept trying to dodge me while making silly faces.

'Will you stop being a dumbhead and give Sonny his keys back?' said Elliot.

'Yeah, just give them back!' I thundered.

'No chance.' Parvin smirked.

I exhaled a breath and decided I wasn't going to stress myself about the situation. So I just stared coolly at

Parvin, not saying anything which made him look a little unnerved.

'Don't you want these keys then?' he said, still holding them above his head.

I shrugged, then looked past him – and gasped.

'Oh no, will you look at that?' I said, pointing towards the far end of the playground.

'What?' replied Parvin looking over his shoulder.

I automatically dived forward to grab my keys, only I was too slow as Parvin backed away immediately.

'Ha, you thought I fell for your trick, didn't you?' He laughed as I rubbed my face in frustration.

He jangled my keys again to taunt me, but I was determined to remain completely calm.

'You're the biggest idiot at this school, do you know that?' I said to him.

'Yeah, yeah,' Parvin mocked.

All of a sudden the maddest thing happened. I had a buzzing sound in my head, then, to my shock, my keys shot straight out of Parvin's hand and into mine.

Parvin's face looked how I'd imagine a face to look if, for instance, the Tooth Fairy, Father Christmas and the Easter Bunny really did exist, and you saw them having a conversation in the playground.

'Are you hiding a magnet or something?' he asked me.

'No,' I replied, 'and you had better hope you've not damaged my keys,' I warned.

Parvin and Zeki walked off, with Parvin still looking flummoxed. All the while I hadn't noticed how startled Elliot was looking.

'Did you … make those keys … fly out of his hand like that?' he asked, his mouth wide open.

'I did tell you I have superpowers,' I replied jubilantly.

CHAPTER 9

'Why do you keep staring at the ketchup like that?' asked Ramona while we were eating dinner.

'I'm reading the label,' I replied, my eyes and my mind fixed on the bottle. But really, I was seeing if I could make it move. Only nothing was happening.

'I didn't realise the ingredients were so fascinating to you, Sonny,' said Dad, munching on a home-made fish finger. Before she left for Jordan, Mum had made a big batch of fish fingers, as she knows how much we love them.

'I never knew ketchup contained so much more than tomatoes,' I said, and stopped focusing on the bottle. Then, quickly, I began to wolf down the remaining food on my plate.

'Fizzy lemons, Sonny! Are you going for a world record, eating so fast?' said Dad.

'I need to start my homework,' I told him, my mouth stuffed full. Once I'd finished my last chip, fish finger and pea, I excused myself from the table and went up to my room.

But it wasn't homework I was planning to do. I was going to test out my powers, and this time I was going to do all that I could to make them work. When I made my keys shoot out of Parvin's hand today, I was fully determined to get them back. So maybe that's what my powers needed – sheer determination.

Sitting down at my desk, I carefully began to focus my mind on all the stuff that was on it – my pens and pencils, my globe, my water bottle, my space rocket, my maths exercise book and my laptop.

'Come on, something just move?!' I said frustratedly, after ten minutes of serious concentration. I was feeling determined, but my determination wasn't making any difference. Nor did I have that buzzing sound in my head that I'd had before whenever I made something move with my mind. I sighed and flopped down on to my bed.

Just what did I need to do to get my superpowers to appear?

I folded my arms and stared up at the ceiling. To be honest, I wasn't surprised my superpowers were being unreliable, because things not working out as they should has pretty much been the story of my life. For example, every birthday I've had for the last four years, my mum has either been away working or was unable to stay for the full duration because she had to jet off to another film shoot, just like she did at my twelfth birthday party. In comparison, Ramona and Oscar have been way luckier. Mum has yet to miss any of their birthdays.

Then there have been the times when I've been really excited about something, like a school trip, and it just doesn't happen because I've got ill, or the weather has been atrocious or some other disaster strikes. Back when I was in Year Four, my class were all set to go to a planetarium which had just opened, and for weeks I'd been looking forward to it. I've always loved learning about the planets and space, so to me it was going to be the best school trip ever. Only, we didn't get to go on the trip due to the rickety old minibus breaking down before we'd even departed. So the trip ended up being cancelled. I sighed again at this memory.

I suppose I should be thankful that I even have superpowers. For all I know, I might be the only person in the world who has powers, which I guess would make me super special!

I smiled this time, which helped me feel a lot less wound up. I thought again of how I managed to get my keys off Parvin. I'd stayed calm, and in my head I'd pictured the keys coming back to me. So maybe that was something else I needed to do – imagine myself moving the object. I briefly closed my eyes as I thought about an item in my room. Suddenly I had a buzzing sound in my head. I quickly opened my eyes to see my globe hovering above me just as I wanted it to.

Finally!

I gazed at the floating globe in amazement. I began to take some slow and deep breaths to make my mind and body feel calmer and all Zen, like Mum does when she's doing her yoga exercises. My head continued to buzz as I concentrated on the globe, imagining it spinning in front of me – and sure enough, it began to do just that.

I looked at a fluffy Power Piglet on one of my bookshelves, which Oscar had annoyingly left in my room. Once again, I kept my breathing slow and steady as I focused my mind on the toy and imagined it flying. Suddenly, the Power Piglet began to judder. I maintained my focus as it began to tremble twice as much, then leaped into the air, floating like a balloon.

I focused my mind back on the globe and made it spin even faster. Then I switched my focus to my books and comics, all of them rising from the shelves like a flock of birds taking flight. With my mind I made them move in formation, rippling and twirling through the air. I used my powers to move my pillows next, and they hopped about on my bed. It was *marnificent*, which is 'marvellous' and 'magnificent' combined.

I made one of my comics float down to me. It was a Batman comic. With my mind, I made the pages turn by themselves as I found myself wondering, *Could I be a superhero?*

Maybe that's the greatness I was meant for! Except there wasn't much heroic stuff I could do. It's not as if Delmere was like Gotham City, with lots of villains to battle. There was Milo Allerton, I suppose, but I'd hate to battle him when he's even scarier than the Joker and the Penguin combined! And if I'm being honest, I'm just too shy – and I'm not that brave either. So the only heroic things I might be able to do are use my powers to help a kid get their ball down from a tree, or help an old lady get across the street by flying her over to the other side – that's if she doesn't mind being flown.

I needed to use the toilet so I left my room for a few minutes, and when I came back, the objects were still moving. Except, my pillows were now looking like two boxers in a ring as they bounced around each other.

I now needed to make it all stop. So I concentrated my mind again, my eyes glancing at my books and comics, the globe, the Power Piglet and my pillows, but for some reason, they continued to move.

I was focusing even harder now, so much so that my head was beginning to hurt. But none of the items would stop moving and instead all of them came towards where I was standing in the doorway, my pillows jumping off the bed and hopping right up to me. I don't know why but I found myself feeling as scared as I did when Milo Allerton chased me this morning. I took a step back, but the objects came forward.

'Just get back, will you!' I said, then wondered why I was even speaking; it's not as if pillows or books have ears. I stepped back again but the objects crept forward.

'Can't you just do as I ask?' I pleaded with my pillows, bending down and patting one of them as though it were a puppy. But the pillows looked FURIOUS, and please don't ask me how inanimate objects can look furious. They just did.

In fact, my pillows looked like they were about to EXPLODE with RAGE, so the only thing I could do was flee.

'AAARGH!!!'

I rushed down the stairs, shrieking my head off, as my books, comics, globe, the Power Piglet and my once snuggly but now psychotic pillows chased after me.

(Now, if you'd told me a month ago that I'd one day find myself running away in terror from a set of pillows and a cuddly toy, I would've wondered if your brain had been surgically removed and replaced with an orange!)

'SWEET MACAROONS!' said Dad, coming into the living room. 'What's all that screaming for?'

'I don't know what's happening, Dad?' I whimpered.

'Well, I have a pretty good idea,' he replied, his eyes glowering. 'Just look at this mess!'

I turned round to see my books and comics scattered across the floor along with the globe, the pillows and the Power Piglet.

'SONNY!' Dad's voice rumbled like a ferocious thundercloud.

'*Sorry,*' was all I could say.

CHAPTER 10

Mum was not happy when she saw the state of the living room when we all had a FaceTime call with her later that evening, Dad panning the iPad around the room so she could take a good look at the 'destruction', as Ramona called it. Trust my sister to have made it seem worse than it was *and* used it as an opportunity to show off her spelling skills.

'D-e-s-t-r … u-c-t-o … I mean … t-i-o-n!' she declared.

Mum clapped and gave her a big smile, which quickly turned back into a big frown as she looked at me from the screen.

'What in heaven possessed you to throw your books about like they're pieces of litter?' she said.

The thing was, I didn't feel ready to tell her or Dad about my superpowers when right now my powers weren't feeling that super. I clearly had a lot to figure out, like how to bring my powers under control and stop them from turning on me. I still couldn't believe I narrowly avoided getting beaten up by my own pillows!

'I brought my books and comics down because I wanted to sort them all into alphabetic order and I brought my pillows as well because I wanted to sit on them while I did this. Plus, I wanted to give Oscar his Power Piglet back and show him and Ramona where Jordan was on the globe,' was the long-winded fib I gave to both Mum and Dad. Luckily my parents bought it. But they still weren't happy with me.

The same went for Oscar, who was sticking plasters all over his Power Piglet as if it had sustained real injuries, while simultaneously sticking his tongue out at me.

'You really need to take better care of your things, Sonny,' said Mum, 'and this had better not happen again!'

'It won't, Mum, I promise.'

'Can we just change the subject now?' said Dad. 'So, Bev, how's the shoot going?' he asked Mum.

'It's going well. I'm really enjoying working with the team again,' she replied.

'But when are you going to come home?' whined Oscar.

We were all missing her so much.

'It still won't be for a while, but when I do get home, I'm going to give all of you the biggest hug ever,' said Mum.

After we chatted to Mum some more, which was mostly Oscar telling her about the latest episode he'd watched of *The Power Piglets* and Ramona spelling out a list of words like 'guarantee' and 'recommendation', it was time for us to say goodbye.

When I was ready to go to bed, I couldn't help feeling a little apprehensive that things in my room might start moving again all by themselves. So it took me a while to get off to sleep, especially as I kept checking my pillows to make sure they hadn't come to life and were about to attack me.

Eventually I fell asleep. I don't remember what I was dreaming about but I do remember I had a tingly sensation in my arms and legs. Then suddenly I was on my street, and I *definitely* wasn't still dreaming. But before I'd even got the chance to get my head around the fact that I was standing in the middle of the road staring straight into the headlights of a car, my body started tingling again and a moment later I was on a trampoline in a garden that I instantly knew was our neighbours' at number 23, Mr and Mrs Okaru. They're good friends with my mum and dad, and we've been to their house plenty of times. Their daughter Blessing is also best friends with Ramona.

Another light flashed in my eyes – the Okarus' security light. I squinted to protect my eyes from the glare as the sound of barking came from inside the house. I began to panic.

Although the Okarus were good friends with my parents, I'd expect they'd be terribly cross if they thought I'd broken into their garden. But it was too late for me to escape as lights started coming on in the house. I quickly jumped down from the trampoline, landing in something VERY cold and VERY smelly, but I didn't have time to worry about that as I crawled under the trampoline to hide.

Mr Okaru came outside with his dog, Noodle, and as Mr Okaru went to inspect the back gate, Noodle sniffed around the garden. It didn't take her long to spot me, her eyes glowing in the dark. She quickly raced over, and I froze, thinking I was about to be savaged, as Noodle was a very large bullmastiff. But thankfully she recognised me and started licking my face.

'*Shh*, Noodle!' I said as she barked in excitement. Immediately Mr Okaru turned round and warily began walking towards us.

'Who's there, Noodle?' he whispered as my panic grew.

I was so going to get into trouble!

But without even trying to teleport away, automatically my body began to tingle, then I was back home, lying flat on the upstairs landing. I sat up. I could still smell the thing that I'd stepped in, and I didn't need to guess what it was – dog poo.

YUCK!

As I tiptoed to the bathroom to wash my smelly feet, I breathed out a heavy sigh of relief. I mean, I wouldn't have liked to have seen the look on Mr Okaru's face had he caught me, or the mortified look I know I would've got from my dad.

My powers *so* weren't playing fair. I needed to find a way to fix them, and fix them fast – otherwise it wouldn't just be dog mess I'd be having to deal with.

CHAPTER 11

I was pleased the next day was Saturday as it meant I could spend some time trying to get a handle on my powers. For the morning at least I was free from any distractions as Dad had taken Oscar and Ramona swimming. So first up was testing my powers of telekinesis.

I knew I could move objects, but could I move and manipulate matter?

In the kitchen, I lined up three empty glasses on the counter. Into the first glass I poured some water. I relaxed my mind and imagined what I wanted the water to do. As a buzzing sound emerged in my head, like a firework the water shot up into the air and poured down into the second glass.

I grinned.

Next, I made the water from the second glass lift and pour into the third glass, and as I maintained my focus, I made the water move from glass to glass, rising and falling like a dragon made of liquid. It was *astrobulous*!

I looked around the kitchen. I hadn't had my breakfast yet and I fancied some Rice Krispies and beans on toast. I pictured everything in my head that I wanted to move, my brain buzzing like a full hive of bees as I opened the cupboard door with my powers and made a can of beans fly out, except a little too fast for me to catch. The can fell and spun across the floor. The box of Rice Krispies came out next, but I was able to slow down its speed by slowing down my thoughts. I directed the box towards me, and it carefully touched down on the kitchen table.

I took a spoon from a drawer, and out of another cupboard I took a bowl, and then got a carton of almond milk from the fridge – all with my mind, of course. All of them floated over to the table. Then, as I concentrated on the box of cereal, I made it tip and pour the Rice Krispies into the bowl, but too many came out and overflowed on to the table. With my powers, I made each of those puffs rise and come together as they swirled and rolled, spiralled and looped, in a thrilling aerial display. Once I'd guided the Rice Krispies back into the box, I made the milk put on a performance too. And seriously,

I never knew milk could be so entertaining! I had it swishing and swilling through the air before it cascaded down into the bowl like a waterfall.

I made my beans on toast next, my mind gently picking up the can of beans and cracking open the lid. And once I'd poured the beans into a saucepan, my mind turned on the cooker to heat it. The bread came out of the cupboard and landed in my arms. I took out two slices, this time with my actual hands, but I threw them up in the air and watched as the slices found their way to the toaster and plopped straight in. It was great how I was managing to do all these things, and I was very pleased that nothing had turned on me.

I looked back at the box of Rice Krispies and wondered if I could crush it with my mind, imagining it all squashed up. I then began to focus, and slowly but surely, the box started to scrunch together.

Could I do this with metals? I wondered.

I looked in one of the cupboards, and from the back I pulled out an empty metal tin. My brain buzzed and my face tightened as I concentrated once again, and not before long, little dents started to appear all around the tin and in the lid. Then the whole tin began to squeeze together until it was all crushed up.

My powers were truly MIND-BLOWING!

As I finally made a start on eating my breakfast I

wondered if I could move things that weren't nearby. I soon put this to the test by picturing our TV in my mind, and as I began to concentrate, all of a sudden I could hear the TV playing in the living room.

It worked!

And then I made the TV get louder, imagining myself turning up the volume. I sprinted to the living room and flicked the TV on to the news by using my mind instead of the remote. Unlike Mrs Armstrong, the news wasn't something I particularly enjoyed watching, but I had an idea. I wanted to see if my powers were strong enough to move things that were even further away. A newsreader was on the screen, and I could see there were sheets of paper on his desk. I pictured what I wanted to do. Then, keeping my mind focused, I made all the papers fly up into the air like they were being blown about by a gust of wind. The newsreader looked completely stunned. Though he wasn't half as stunned as me, knowing that I could move things from a great distance and right now I was doing it on live TV!

'Not quite sure what's going on here,' said the news-reader, trying to keep his voice composed as I brought the papers back down on to the desk and shuffled them into a neat pile. The newsreader quickly leaped up from his seat.

'Who's doing this?! Is this some sort of prank?' he said, as he walked round in front of the desk and then walked out of shot. The camera followed and you could see he was muttering something to someone who I guessed might've been a producer. The newsreader looked very angry.

Uh-oh!

It hadn't been my intention to cause havoc. But I guess you could say I was making the news, except no one knew.

The newsreader returned to the desk and sat back down cautiously.

'Apologies for that slight interruption. In other news, the construction of a new multimillion-pound bridge has been given the green light—'

I switched off the TV.

At least I'd managed to make the boring news a bit more interesting today!

CHAPTER 12

I decided to be even more daring and move something big. The largest thing in the living room was the sofa, and without any difficulty I was able to lift it with my mind and keep it suspended in the air. I made it rock from side to side like a boat on a choppy sea and spin right around, before I decided it was time for me to test my flying skills. With my eyes closed, I carefully focused my mind.

'You can fly, Sonny, you can fly!' I said, as though giving myself a pep talk.

I took a deep breath as I willed my body to move. A few seconds later, my feet began to lift from the floor, and I was floating up to the sofa. I sat down and looked below.

It's surprising how much you notice when you've got a new perspective on things. That was something my mum liked to say. Being so high up certainly gave me a new perspective on the living room. There were a few things I hadn't properly noticed before or realised were even there. For instance, it had never occurred to me that my parents had colour-coordinated a set of patterned plates on the wall, a red pattern followed by a green pattern followed by another red pattern and then a second green patterned plate.

I finally found where an old Hot Wheels car of mine had got to, which was on top of our tall oak-panelled cabinet. I'm not sure how the car had got up there – unless Dad had put it there, as he was the only one who could reach that high.

I flew out of the room and into the hall. For me, flying is the best superpower there could ever be, so I was really living my best life!

I was still to test my ability to teleport, which was something I really needed to get to grips with, as I'd hate to find myself in the middle of the road again or in one of our neighbours' gardens.

I decided that, for now, I'd keep my teleportation nice and simple as I pictured my chosen destination – my bedroom. Only, nothing was happening. There was no tingly feeling in my body, and I was still in the hall. I tried to concentrate harder while keeping my breathing slow and steady. A moment later, a tingly sensation began to flow through me, then in a bat of an eye, I was in my bedroom.

I was super pleased my teleporting had worked, and now I was ready to teleport myself to somewhere further away. After grabbing some money I began to concentrate, my thoughts homing in on the place I wanted to be. My arms and legs started to tingle, then I was gone.

CHAPTER 13

Faster than a snap of the fingers, I was standing in my favourite ice-cream parlour, which also happened to be the only ice-cream parlour in Delmere. It was called Ice To Meet You and they did the best dairy-free cookie-dough ice cream I've ever tasted. Plus, they did delicious waffles and an amazing blueberry slushie.

Even though it was only eleven thirty, the place was rammed. So I don't think anyone noticed me miraculously appearing in front of the toilets at the back. I went up to the counter and smiled shyly at a girl who was pouring out slushies. Her name was Delilah Buckley and she was in my form at school. The ice-cream parlour was owned by Delilah's parents, and she sometimes helped them out. They did pay her though, so in a way it was like a proper job.

'Hi, what would you like?' said a man behind the counter – Delilah's dad.

'I'll have a cookie-dough ice cream please,' I told him.

'Cup or cone?'

'Cone please.'

Mr Buckley nodded and began to scoop out the ice cream from the tub inside the glass display.

'Is that ice cream your breakfast?' asked Delilah as her dad handed me my cookie-dough ice cream.

'No, I've already had my breakfast,' I said, and I could feel my voice quivering a bit. 'So I guess you could call this an early lunch.'

I always felt shy and dorky around girls, and Delilah was no exception. But she was the only girl who made my hands feel fizzy whenever I spoke to her.

'See you at school,' I said, as I walked out licking my ice cream. I was enjoying it so much that at first I didn't realise someone was tapping me on the shoulder.

'Am I glad to see you,' said the voice, as I turned round and looked up at the nasty, grinning face of Milo Allerton.

SPLAT!!!

Without giving me the chance to even say hello, Milo had WHACKED my ice cream out of my hand, and it fell to the ground with a big *slop*.

'You're that Year Seven who used our entrance yesterday,' he snarled. 'I was looking for you but couldn't find you.'

'Well, you've found him now,' said his friend Aiden.

I gulped.

'So, you got anything to say for yourself?' barked Milo.

'I'm sorry, I won't use the path again,' I quickly murmured.

'Yeah, you'd better not,' Milo warned, then looked at my ice cream on the ground. He smirked. 'Shame you'll have to buy another ice cream, but that's what you get for not following the rules!'

'I will from now on. I swear,' I rasped, as the boys barged past me into the ice-cream parlour.

I looked again at my poor ice cream on the pavement but concluded it could've been *a lot* worse. At least I managed not to get my face smashed in. But I couldn't help feeling a little sorry for myself and I just wanted to get home. Trouble was, it wasn't going to be easy teleporting myself back home in the middle of a busy street. So I walked back instead and came to a decision: I was going to tell Dad about my superpowers. Maybe that would make things a little easier.

When I got in, Dad, Ramona and Oscar were back from the swimming pool and were sitting in the conservatory. I joined them and the first thing I said was, 'Dad, I have something to tell you.'

'And I have something to tell *you*,' he replied, and I couldn't quite work out from the expression on his face if I was in trouble or not. I did leave the kitchen in a bit of a mess from testing out my powers, so maybe he wanted to tell me off for that. Except it turned out I wasn't in any trouble at all.

'How would you like to do some babysitting this evening?' said Dad, his face breaking into a smile.

'Babysitting?' I repeated.

'Yes, babysitting your brother and sister. I was hoping Mrs Armstrong would do it as per usual, but she says she's feeling a little under the weather.'

To tell you I was shocked would be an understatement! My parents have never let me babysit before, and up until now, they were convinced *I* still needed babysitting.

'I'm doing a shorter shift this evening, so it'll just be for a few hours,' said Dad.

My dad wasn't acting in anything at the moment so he was working as a food delivery courier. My dad's actually what you call a 'jobbing actor', which means he does other stuff as well. He's had lots of interesting jobs over the years: office receptionist, telemarketer, waiter, shop assistant, street fundraiser, cinema assistant and nightclub bouncer. He wore a very cool suit for that last job.

'And you really think I'm responsible enough to babysit?' I asked.

'Yes, I do, Sonny.'

I pretended to think about his offer, though the answer was always going to be 'YES!'

'OK, I'll babysit.'

'I only want him babysitting me if we can watch *Encanto*,' said Ramona.

'Haven't you watched that film a dozen times already?' said Dad.

'But it's my favourite film, I *have* to watch it,' Ramona replied.

'It's no problem, we can watch *Encanto* if you want,' I said.

Dad put on his serious face again. 'Now, I don't want you proving me wrong, Sonny, that you can be responsible. So I don't want to come back to this house and find it in a sorry state.'

'You won't, Dad. Don't worry,' I assured him.

'I want to feel I can trust you, and if you do a good job then I might let you babysit again.'

'I will get paid for this, won't I?'

Dad lowered his glasses. 'The plan was I'd pay you with a pizza, then afterwards I thought we could bring down your telescope and do some stargazing in the garden. It's been a while since we've done that, and you never know, we might just make some extraterrestrial discoveries!'

'Cool!' I replied.

Pizza and stargazing with Dad were two of my favourite things. I'm always hoping that I'll get to see signs of alien life out there in the cosmos. I've not spotted any signs as yet, but I still believe aliens exist. Sometimes I wonder if they're looking through telescopes of their own, right back at us.

'I'm also willing to add an extra five pounds to your pocket money for this week. How does that sound?' said Dad.

'Brilliant!' I grinned. 'Thanks, Dad.'

So as I got to work in showing my dad just how responsible I could be, my plan of telling him I had superpowers somehow slipped my mind. Even before Dad left for work, I was doing all I could to impress him by cleaning the kitchen and tidying my bedroom and Oscar's room too. I left Ramona's room as she has this big sign on her door that says:

KEEP OUT!
Particcularly big and little brothers

There were two stick figures drawn next to this, one big and one small, that had a large X drawn over them. I did complain at how offensive the sign was and Mum and Dad agreed, except they were more offended that Ramona had spelt *particularly* with two cs. My sister also refused to take the sign down or at least be bothered to correct the spelling mistake.

Lastly, I cleaned the bathroom, though I did cheat a bit by using my mind to control the sponge as I scrubbed the sink and bath.

'Crusty breadcrumbs! I've never seen the kitchen so clean, and the bathroom is practically gleaming!' said Dad, looking MEGA impressed. 'Are you sure this is my house?' he joked. He gave me a smile that was more sparkling than the bathtub. 'Do you know what? I think I'll add ten pounds to your pocket money this week.'

For a second, I wondered if Dad was still joking, but when he grabbed his wallet and put a crisp ten-pound note in my hand and said, 'I'm very proud of you, Stupendous Sonny,' that moment felt more special than my superpowers.

CHAPTER 14

DISASTER!!!

That's basically how my evening of babysitting went. I stupidly thought it would be easy-peasy lemon-squeezy, but no, it turned out to be a TERRIBLE NIGHTMARE! And when Dad returned home, the pride that had shone brightly in his eyes towards me just a few hours earlier had disintegrated into total anger.

It had all kicked off shortly after Dad had left for work. I really should've known Ramona and Oscar were plotting something from the sneaky looks on their faces. We hadn't managed to finish the pizzas Dad had ordered from our favourite pizza restaurant, Big Sal's, so there were still several slices left. And the minute I put the film *Encanto* on, the words 'FOOD FIGHT!' rang out, and Ramona and Oscar were throwing pizza at one another.

Now, things wouldn't have been so bad had their aim been any good, but they kept missing each other, meaning there were slices of pizza splattered on the walls, the armchairs and even the television, leaving splodges of tomato sauce with bits of pepperoni.

Then they decided to have a 'WATER FIGHT!' and ran to the kitchen, filling up cups of water, but again their aim was appalling, so there were puddles all over the kitchen floor, and on the carpet when they took their fight through to the rest of the house. Worst of all, they threw water all over Dad's Constable painting that hung in the hall.

It wasn't a genuine Constable, who was an artist who lived hundreds of years ago, because the real paintings are supposed to be dead expensive. It was just a poster Dad had bought from a car boot sale and got framed. The picture was of a field, which in my opinion was properly dull, but Dad said it reminded him of a field in the village of Shillbrook where he grew up. Therefore the poster meant a lot to him, so I could bet all the pennies in my piggy bank that he wouldn't be happy to find it half destroyed. But Ramona and Oscar just wouldn't listen to me when I kept telling them to stop messing about.

And because I didn't have the kind of powers that allowed me to be in two places at once, while I was downstairs trying to dry the poster with Mum's hairdryer, my brother and sister were upstairs wrecking everything in sight! I was livid, and when I stormed upstairs, it looked like there had been a riot! The bathroom sink was overflowing and there were white feathers covering the floor, due to Ramona and Oscar busting open Mum and Dad's goose feather pillows. There were hand paint-prints on the walls because Oscar had decided to get out his paint pots, and his room, which I'd carefully tidied up earlier, was now messier than a rubbish dump.

'You two are in so much trouble!' I fumed as they jumped up and down on Oscar's bed.

'Not as much trouble as you're going to be in,' said Ramona gleefully.

'You've done this on purpose, haven't you?'

'Daddy should've given us ten pounds,' said Oscar.

'Yeah, it's not fair he gave you that money,' said Ramona.

'So you're jealous. That's why you did this?'

But I didn't have time to argue. I had to get the place looking clean and tidy again before Dad got back. So I did my best to mop up all the water, and then I got scrubbing, by hand, the paint off the walls. All the while, Ramona and Oscar looked on with grins on their faces.

Then, annoyingly, much earlier than I'd expected, Dad returned home.

'SMOKY BACON!' he yelled, and when Dad said this particular phrase, you just knew you were about to be in the worst trouble possible. The first time I heard my dad say this phrase was when he found a hole in a shirt after taking it to the dry cleaner's. The second time was when I was eight after I'd got into a fight with Parvin over a bag of jelly beans. They were my jelly beans which Parvin had tried to snatch from me, marking the start of him becoming my arch-nemesis.

'What's happened to my Constable?' Dad asked as I lumbered slowly down the stairs. Even though the poster wasn't as wet as before, it was sort of lumpy.

But before I could explain, Dad went charging around the house, pointing out the terrible state of everything.

'Just look at this! And that! And this! The place looks like a complete tip!'

'It was all Oscar and Ramona, Dad. They made this mess,' I told him.

'But you were supposed to be looking after your brother and sister, not allowing them to cause pande-monium! I trusted you, Sonny, and you've let me down,' he said, shaking his head at me, which made me feel like bursting into tears even though I rarely cry. 'Well, you won't be babysitting them again, that I can tell you. Plus, I'll be stopping your pocket money for at least a month. The money can go towards some new pillows for me and your mum. And I want back the ten pounds I gave to you.'

'But we can still do some stargazing, can't we?' I asked, which made Dad look at me as if I'd said a swear word.

'Definitely not,' he replied, shaking his head again.

I knew Dad was angry with me but he'd never said no to stargazing before.

'I'm just too disappointed with you to do that right now,' he added.

So yes, my first time as a babysitter had been a COLOSSAL DISASTER. Not only that, but I was also ten quid down.

CHAPTER 15

Dad being so cross and disappointed with me made me feel miserable. I tried to do more cleaning, but this just annoyed Dad even more. I think it was because I was using a scouring pad to clean the walls, and I ended up scrubbing off some of the paintwork in places.

'Look, I'll tidy everything up, you just get to bed,' he said snippily once he'd texted Mum to tell her what had happened, and I just knew she was going to be disappointed with me too.

And once again, the telling-off Ramona and Oscar received was nowhere near as bad as mine. They didn't have to hear their pocket money was being stopped. The only thing Dad said was that he never wanted them making a mess of the house again, and they agreed they wouldn't. Not that I believed them. And because I was feeling down at how the evening had gone, it was hard for me to get off to sleep. After tossing and turning several times, I spent a while watching funny dog and cat videos on YouTube. Only, the videos weren't enough to cheer me up, but I did know something that could – my superpowers!

Getting out of bed, I put on my trainers and pulled on my jacket over my pyjamas, then snuck out of my room and went downstairs. As I opened the front door, I left it on the latch before going outside. My eyes glanced at the houses that were all in darkness and at the cars that lined the street, including our own car. I peered at a van that belonged to our next-door neighbour at number 24, Mr Donohue. He collects scrap metal, and his van was always full of the stuff. The van probably weighed a tonne.

Could I lift it? I wondered.

I'd lifted the sofa with my mind and that was pretty heavy, but lifting a van would definitely be a step up. I took a deep breath as I began to fix all my concentration on the van, my brain buzzing away. Very slowly, the van began to rock from side to side. I concentrated harder, my eyes narrowing at the intensity. Then without delay, the van started to rise up and up until it must have been about ten metres in the air.

I smiled brightly, and it was as if I'd been lifted as well, even though my feet were firmly on the ground. I focused my mind on the other vehicles next, and one by one they too began to rise. I soon had them all moving up and down in the sky like musical notes on a page, and it felt as if the cars were performing a silent concerto. I flew up to our roof and sat down to watch this *marnificent* spectacle. I wish my dad could've seen the cars. I should've just told him about my superpowers as I'd planned. I wasn't feeling so upset any more. In fact, I couldn't have felt happier.

I flew back down, focusing my mind again as I brought down the cars and Mr Donohue's van. It should've been easy, but they all came down with an ALMIGHTY CLANG!!! All at once, lights turned on in every house, including mine. I quickly sprinted back inside, hoping no one had seen me.

Dad came running down the stairs as Ramona and Oscar peered over the landing, rubbing their sleepy eyes.

'I guess that must've woken you up as well. It sounded like an explosion!' said Dad, striding past me and heading out.

I followed. Lots of our neighbours had gathered on the street, their coats over their nighties and pyjamas, all of them trying to figure out what had happened.

'I just heard a horrendous bang!' said Miss Lister at number 31.

'It frightened my whole family out of our skin,' said Mrs Moretti at number 26.

'What do you think it might've been?' said Mr Okaru to another neighbour, Mr Goodwin at number 19.

'I haven't a clue, Kofi. All I know is that I'm probably not going to get much sleep now,' huffed Mr Goodwin.

My street was one of those streets where everyone knows everyone, which Dad said was increasingly rare nowadays. I don't know all the jobs my neighbours do but I did know that Miss Lister was a business analyst, Mrs Moretti was an interior designer, and Mr Okaru was an optometrist who my family went to whenever we needed an eye test. His wife, Mrs Okaru, worked in advertising. Then there was Mr Goodwin, who's my history teacher. As much as I liked my road, it was dead annoying having to live on the same street as one of my teachers.

Mrs Armstrong came over to us in her furry red slippers.

'Ah, my heart! That noise was so loud. Do you know what it was?' she said, clutching her chest, which made me feel guilty.

'Hey, there's a DENT in my car!' Mr Okaru suddenly cried.

'Hang on a minute, there's a DENT in my van!' said Mr Donohue, shaking his head.

'My car bumper is WRECKED!' yelled Mrs Moretti.

'It'll be some yobbos no doubt, and that noise was probably them trying to smash everything up!' said Miss Roland at number 14.

Everyone seemed so cross, which just made me feel even more guilty.

'At least our car looks OK,' said Dad as I joined him to inspect it. 'But whoever those yobs are, I hope they get what's coming to them!' he added.

And of course, he wouldn't have been pleased to know that the 'yob' was me. There was no way I could tell Dad about my superpowers now, because instead of being proud of me as I hoped he would be, after tonight's mayhem I expect he'd only be even more furious with me.

CHAPTER 16

Elliot couldn't believe his ears when I told him about my weekend as we walked to school on Monday. I went through in detail how I'd teleported myself to Ice To Meet You and how I got my ice cream bashed in, and almost my head, by Milo Allerton. Of course, Elliot was stunned beyond words when I explained how I was able to move things just by thinking about them and how I'd moved the papers on the newsreader's desk and lifted the cars on my road.

'Wow! You seriously have to show me all the stuff you can do,' he said excitedly.

'Well, I can tonight when I come over.'

'Ace! Though it's probably best you don't use your powers to lift our sofa as I don't think my parents would appreciate it.' He giggled. 'But it's good to hear you're not having much difficulty in getting your powers to work now.'

'It has been taking a lot of practice, but yeah, I think I've finally got the hang of it.'

Suddenly something occurred to me. 'Oh no, I forgot the game!'

'It's OK, we can play one of my games tonight,' said Elliot.

'But I promised to bring it, and seriously, Elliot, it's one of the best video games I've ever played.'

I'd arranged to go to Elliot's house for dinner, and the plan was we'd play the video game that my parents had got me as a birthday present. It was called *Intergalactic Assignment* and was about a boy who must survive life on different planets as part of a literally out-of-this-world homework project.

'Duh!' I said, slapping my forehead. 'I could just teleport myself home at break and get the game. It'll take me less than a minute, so no one will even notice that I've gone.'

So when the bell went for break at ten past eleven, Elliot and I headed to the boys' toilets. I went into one of the cubicles and Elliot stood outside, pretending he was waiting to use the toilet, so that we didn't bring attention to ourselves. Closing my eyes, I pictured my bedroom in my mind, but when I opened my eyes I was still in the cubicle and there was no tingly sensation in my arms and legs. I tried again, thinking of all the things that were in my room, including the video game which I'd left on my desk, but for some odd reason, I couldn't teleport.

Maybe I'm not calm enough, I thought.

I had just had a rather stressful maths lesson where I failed to solve a difficult sum in front of the class. My teacher, Miss Kerrigan, nominated me to come up, even though there were other kids with their hands up, including Elliot, who's a maths genius. I swear the teachers love picking me to answer questions on the board. Maybe it's something they all plot together in the staffroom.

As I struggled to work out the sum, I could hear Parvin and Zeki laughing, which made my cheeks feel hot and my hand start to shake, which made my writing go all wibbly-wobbly.

'That's not correct, but well done for trying, Sonny,' said Miss Kerrigan, taking the pen from me as I skulked back to my seat.

'Are you back yet?' Elliot whispered through the door, snapping me out of the memory of my embarrassing maths lesson.

'I've not actually left,' I whispered back. 'Just give me a minute.'

I began breathing in and out slowly to relax, then I tried one last time to teleport home, but nothing happened. So I had no choice but to give up.

I clicked open the door and shook my head at Elliot.

'What happened?' he asked as we headed out of the toilets.

'It didn't work. I couldn't teleport,' I said with a frown.

'How come?'

I shrugged. 'Maybe I'm just not in the right frame of mind right now. I'll try again at lunchtime.'

But when lunchtime came, once again I failed to teleport. It seemed my powers had gone back to being unreliable.

'It looks like I'm going to have to walk back home after school and get the game. Then I'll get the bus to your place,' I told Elliot resignedly.

So, at the end of school, I went straight home and once I'd changed out of my uniform and grabbed the video game, I headed back out. The bus arrived just as I reached the stop, and once I'd hopped on, I sent Elliot a text message to let him know I was on my way.

Two stops after mine, a boy who I was sure goes to my school got on, with a girl who I guessed was his sister as they looked alike, and they both sat in the seats in front of me. I think the boy was either a Year Ten or

Eleven, but I didn't know his name and I don't think he'd been at my school for long. He had earphones in, and was bopping his head, while his sister was drawing a picture in a sketchbook. I snuck a peek, curious as to what she was drawing, and it turned out to be a helter-skelter. I've never been on a helter-skelter. I'm more your roller-coaster kind of kid, except for the ones that go upside down.

'Nice picture,' I said to the girl, and she immediately closed her sketchbook.

She turned her head round.

'Thanks,' she replied in a quiet voice.

I smiled, then pressed the bell for my stop.

As the bus came to a halt, I got out my phone again, as I wanted to text Elliot to let him know I'd be at his place in five minutes. But when I got off the bus, I clumsily dropped my phone, and as I went to pick it up, a familiar buzzing sound filled my head and without me having to even think about it, my phone just lifted straight back into the palm of my hand. I quickly looked around to check that no one had seen this, and feeling certain nobody had, I let out a sigh of relief. It was also a relief to know that at least one aspect of my superpowers was still working.

CHAPTER 17

Elliot lived at the end of a road called Westley Drive. When I reached his house, his sister Willow opened the door and straight away I could hear giggling and saw that it was Elliot's other sister Phoebe, who was hiding behind Willow. Phoebe's two, and everything and anything makes her giggle, including me. As I went inside, I pulled a goofy face which made Phoebe giggle even more.

'Elliot's upstairs,' said Willow. 'And just to let you know, my mum is about to serve dinner, so you've arrived just in time.'

Willow is Elliot's younger sister by ten months, so she's still at primary school. Her school is called Maple Lane and it's where Elliot and I both went. Ramona and

Oscar go there as well. Willow, like her brother, was another brainbox, especially when it came to maths.

'Ramona told me all about the hot-air balloon that landed in your school playground the other week. Did Mr Nelson ever find out who it belonged to?' I asked Willow.

'I don't think so, but that day was really weird. It was like the hot-air balloon just appeared by magic,' she said.

'Ramona was in the school library with her friend Blessing, and said that when they went outside, they couldn't believe their eyes when they saw it.'

'Everyone thinks Mr Nelson has kept the hot-air balloon for himself,' said Willow. 'I wish I owned a hot-air balloon. It'd be so amazing to see what Delmere and other places look like from above.'

I nodded my head in agreement, but I knew that, with my powers, I didn't need any hot-air balloon to do that!

I climbed the stairs to Elliot's room and put my head around the door. 'I've got the game!' I announced.

'Excellent!' he cheered.

'I think my powers might've sorted themselves out because when I was getting off the bus, I dropped my phone, and automatically it came back into my hand.'

'Well, that's good news because I can't wait to see more of your powers for myself,' said Elliot. 'So after dinner, we can go out to the garden and you can show me.'

'Sounds like a plan!'

Elliot's mum had made lasagne for dinner, which was delicious, and she didn't mind me putting lots of tomato ketchup on it, unlike Mrs Armstrong who reckons I spoil her stew when I mix it with ketchup. But to me, ketchup just makes everything taste better.

Afterwards, while Elliot's parents and sisters watched some telly, Elliot and I went out to the garden.

'So which ability do you want to show me first?' said Elliot eagerly. 'And by the way, you don't have to worry about me not keeping it all a secret. I won't tell a soul unless you want me to.'

'Thanks,' I replied, then rubbed my hands together. 'All right, let's get started! I think I'll show you my tele-portation skills first, and fingers crossed it works this time.'

I held up two crossed fingers as I focused my thoughts on where I wanted to go. Very quickly my body started to tingle, and amazingly it worked! I made Elliot jump as I stood behind him and said, 'BOO!'

Elliot looked astounded.

'Y-y-you were over there … but n-n-now you're here,' he said, not quite believing it.

'I have superpowers, what can I say?' I grinned.

'I don't mean to steal one of your dad's phrases, but TANGY CHEESE BALLS, Sonny, that was spectacular!

You actually disappeared, then reappeared!' Elliot exclaimed.

'I'm just glad it worked.'

'How does it feel when you teleport? Does your body feel like it's going all wavy or that blood is rushing to your head?'

'I'd say I feel more tingly than wavy, but that feeling disappears once I've teleported.'

I instantly made myself disappear again, before I reappeared in another part of the garden. I did it again and again, and it became like a game, with Elliot pointing to where he'd think I'd appear, only for me to reappear somewhere else. Then he didn't know where I was when I teleported myself to his roof.

'I'm up here!' I called as I watched him look around bewilderedly.

Elliot glanced up and straight away his face looked worried.

'You could hurt yourself being up there.'

'I'm fine, but I'll come down,' I said.

As I parted my arms, a feeling of excitement rushed through me. Although I was standing on a roof, I truly felt like I was standing on top of the world! I took a deep breath and leaped into the sky. It was such a joyful feeling flying around Elliot's garden, and it was as though the sky belonged to me and me alone. Breathing in the soft breeze, I smiled down at Elliot, who was staring up at me like how toddlers stare at bubbles, in complete fascination. I sped up, skimming the top of Elliot's head, once then twice, before I touched back down.

'You can fly! You can fly!' Elliot said. Then I noticed him looking a bit wobbly, like he was about to pass out and I quickly rushed over to him.

'You all right, bro?'

'I just need to sit down,' he muttered, and I led him over to one of the garden chairs. 'You have to realise this is still a lot to take in. Finding out you have superpowers is one thing, but seeing them … I just … I don't know what to say!'

This made me wonder: when I eventually tell my parents, should I expect a similar reaction? I certainly wouldn't want them fainting!

'I didn't mean to shock you,' I said to Elliot.

'It's OK. I suppose I'm just shocked because it's hardly the kind of thing you see every day, is it? A person flying. But seriously, Sonny, your powers are mega fantastic!' He tapped the arms of the chair. 'So come on then, show me some more. Move something!' he grinned.

I nodded, and as my mind began to buzz, I concentrated on the thing I wanted to move.

'WHOA!' said Elliot, as I lifted the chair he was sitting on.

'If you want me to put you down, I can.'

'No, it's all right. You can even lift me higher,' he said.

So I did.

'It's like *I'm* flying!' He beamed.

Then I moved Elliot around the garden.

'Welcome aboard Sonny Airlines, this is your captain speaking,' I said, my voice muffled as I spoke into my hand. 'I do hope you're enjoying today's flight.'

'I certainly am, Captain!' said Elliot from above.

'Right then, hold on tight – or hold on to something – because this flight is about to get *very* interesting.'

Quickly Elliot gripped hold of the chair arms, then whooped happily as I had him doing loop-de-loops.

After that I made Elliot go round the garden again and again, really fast, like he was in a flying race car, before eventually bringing him back down to earth.

'Now, that was amazing!' he said, giving me a high-five.

CHAPTER 18

'I want to show you something else,' I said to Elliot. 'I hope it will look as *ginomenal* as I think it's going to be.'

Elliot looked intrigued and followed me to his sister Phoebe's sandpit. He watched as I focused on the sand, a buzzing sound emerging in my head once again. All of a sudden, the sand began to rise, creating a wall.

'Wow!' said Elliot, as the sand stood thickly between us. 'I can't even see you,' he added, then walked around the wall.

I focused again as I made the sand create a circle and then rotate rapidly like a spinning wheel. Then I changed the shape of it again as I made it whoosh and whirl around us, before having all the sand drop back into the sandpit.

'I hope you don't mind me pinching another one of your dad's phrases, but SQUASHED TOMATOES, Sonny, that was awesome!'

'I know, right?'

'Where you got these powers from is what I want to know.'

'So would I,' I replied. 'But I don't think I was born with these powers, because up until a few weeks ago, I didn't have any powers whatsoever.'

'Maybe they were lying dormant – you know, sort of like a volcano. So perhaps your powers were just waiting until they could finally come out like lava.'

'Possibly. Though no one in my family has super-powers … At least, I don't think they do.'

'Maybe you're the exception, or maybe there's another mystery to all of this,' said Elliot.

'I'd love to know if there are other people out there with powers.'

'So when do you think you'll tell your parents?' asked Elliot.

'Well, I would've told my dad at the weekend had he not been cross with me, thanks to Ramona and Oscar. So now I'm not quite sure when I'll tell them both. Though I have been thinking how cool it'd be to become everyone's friendly neighbourhood superhero – just like Spider-Man, and with my own secret identity.'

'... As you come to Delmere's rescue!' said Elliot, in a deep voice. 'Sonny Lawson was once just an ordinary boy, but now he's a mighty superhero!'

'So, which of my powers was your favourite?' I said with a smile.

'Definitely your ability to teleport. It's the fact that you can go anywhere in an instant which to me is beyond amazing,' said Elliot.

'I bet you won't guess where I go next?' I challenged him.

'Um, the roof again?'

'Let's just see, shall we?' I smiled and got ready to teleport. Only this time something felt different. Instead of my arms and legs feeling tingly, they felt really, *really* wobbly. Plus, I had a sharp ringing in my ears. I had expected to teleport to the garden shed, but when I reappeared, I wasn't in Elliot's garden or even on his street.

I was nowhere, and all I could see was darkness.

CHAPTER 19

I didn't know if I was even alive.

Was this death?

I was, however, still breathing, so I couldn't have been dead, and the air that I breathed felt like it was puncturing my lungs. It was that COLD!

Maybe I'd travelled to another planet, just like Kenji, who's the main character in *Intergalactic Assignment*, or maybe I was just floating in the infinite darkness of space. And even though I couldn't see my body, I was sure I was floating, because I couldn't feel anything beneath my feet. I also couldn't move my legs or my arms so I couldn't escape!

'HELP!' I screamed as my voice echoed back. 'HELP!'

What if I get stuck here forever? I suddenly thought.

I don't think I could bear life without my family, my video games, my books and comics, my telescope, tomato ketchup, and even Elliot. That's if I didn't freeze to death first.

I felt so scared. I tried moving again, but it was like an invisible force was in control of my body that wasn't letting me move at all. I pictured Elliot's house in my head and focused as hard as I could to teleport myself back there, but I remained stuck. I continued anyway, but after a while, my head began to hurt from all the focusing I was doing.

'Don't cry!' I told myself as tears pooled in my eyes.

I shouted for help again, but once more it was just my voice that echoed back.

Then, without warning, scatterings of light began to pour into the darkness, and I had to squint as my eyes tried to adjust. It was like I was surrounded by blinds which had slightly opened. At first it was really blurry, but like a Polaroid photo from Dad's old camera, the blurriness became clearer, and I could vaguely see what was on the other side. I could see grass, and when I turned my head to the right, I could see wood like a wooden ... SHED! Then I could see someone's stripy top. *Elliot!* I was in Elliot's garden, which confused me because if I was still in his garden, how in the SWEET MACAROONS did I end up in this stuck place?!

'Hey, Elliot, I'm here!' I said, but it was clear Elliot couldn't hear me.

More light scattered in, and I could now see more of the garden, and I could fully see my arms and legs.

'MOVE!' I shouted at my immobile body. Then, after a moment, I began to wobble tremendously fast.

In fact, there was so much wobbling going on, it was like I'd sprouted multiple legs and arms, all wobbling together like stringy cheese! And once the wobbling had stopped, I was able to properly move as I flew down what felt like a corridor of dark nothingness.

I was flying as fast as I could, but more and more of the corridor greeted me. I felt like I'd flown miles, but the corridor just didn't seem to have an end. I stopped suddenly and stared towards the half-light that filtered in. To my surprise, I was still in Elliot's garden. It was well weird. More than an hour or two must have passed, but there was no change in the light outside to suggest the sun was going down.

Was time different in this stuck place?

Maybe I'd crossed into a parallel universe? If so, I was determined to get out. I focused my mind once more as my body started wobbling all over again. Then suddenly I started to fall, like I was being dropped out of the sky. I was surrounded by complete darkness again, and had no idea where I was tumbling down to.

Was I about to go somewhere worse than this place?

I couldn't imagine anywhere being worse than where I already was. I tried to fly back up, but the invisible force was pulling me down. Then, randomly, with a soft landing, I found myself back in Elliot's garden.

'You're back! Where did you go?' said Elliot, looking baffled.

'I don't know,' I muttered to him, confused myself. 'How long have I been gone?'

'A few minutes.'

'Really? I felt like I've been gone for hours,' I said, standing up. 'It was so strange. Just before I teleported, my body went all wobbly, which has never happened before.'

'You definitely weren't wobbling. You looked fine to me,' said Elliot.

'Well, maybe it was just my insides that were wobbling. Anyway, I don't know where this place was that I went to. It looked like I was still here in the garden, but for ages I couldn't move. I was just floating. Plus, the whole place was completely black. I seriously thought I was going to be stuck there forever!'

'That's strange. I thought you'd teleported to the shed, but when I looked inside, you weren't there.'

'Well, the shed was where I was planning to go.'

'I thought you'd teleported somewhere else

entirely,' said Elliot. 'I didn't realise you were still in my garden!'

I sighed. 'I do like having superpowers, but seriously, if they were something I bought in a shop, I guarantee you I'd be asking for my money back.'

For the first time, I felt quite fearful of my powers.

What was that stuck place? What if I found myself there again? And what if I couldn't get back, not ever?

CHAPTER 20

The next day I decided to put some space between myself and my powers, just like how Mum had decided to put some space between herself and her sister, my Auntie Cleo. Well, that's what she called it. And to my mum, putting space between her and my aunt meant stopping invitations to birthday parties, as well as Christmas dinner and weekend stays at our house. It also meant only phoning Auntie Cleo every once in a while. The reason for this was because my mum and my Auntie Cleo had a big row about my dad one Christmas. Auntie Cleo and my dad had never got on. She was always criticising him and I think it was because she didn't like that he was a jobbing actor, and all that tension between them had just been building and building until my mum finally felt she had to say something. She told Auntie Cleo to get out of our house and never come back, and that was the last I saw of Auntie Cleo. My mum and Auntie Cleo have sort of made up, but my mum still wants to keep some space between them. Well, that's what I heard her say to Dad recently.

I told myself I wouldn't use my powers for at least a few days because they clearly weren't working as they should. You could even say my powers were poorly, which meant they needed a good rest and lots of chicken soup. Though, in my reality, it'd more likely be lots of chicken stew, courtesy of Mrs Armstrong.

However, from the minute I woke up it was tough trying to resist the urge not to use my powers. For one, it would've been so much easier not having to hold my toothbrush while brushing my teeth, and it would've been helpful to have used my powers to do up my tie, which I always find super fiddly and hard to make perfectly straight.

When I went downstairs, Dad had my breakfast waiting at the kitchen table – a bowl of Rice Krispies and an apple. Ramona and Oscar were already at the table eating their breakfast, while Dad was checking his phone.

'Don't forget I'm working this evening, so Mrs Armstrong will be coming over to babysit,' he said in my direction, his eyes still on his phone.

'And no doubt we'll be having chicken stew for dinner,' I said with a sigh.

'There's nothing wrong with Mrs Armstrong's stew,' said Dad, briefly glancing at me. 'It's full of the good stuff – carrots, broad beans, garlic. So I don't want to hear you've been complaining about it, all right?'

'Maybe she'll make us pancakes today,' said Oscar, even though Mrs Armstrong has never made us pancakes before.

'Pancakes are not for dinner. They're for dessert or breakfast,' said Ramona loftily.

'You can have them for dinner actually,' I chipped in.

'No, you can't!' Ramona retorted.

'Yes, you can!' I bit back.

'Kids, no arguing!' said Dad, before bursting out with, 'STICKY MARMALADE! There was a TORNADO in Ocean View!'

'A tornado!' I repeated.

Ocean View was a town next to Delmere.

'Yeah, yesterday,' said Dad, blinking. 'I'm reading a post about it on social media. I can't believe it!'

'Has there ever been a tornado in Ocean View before?' I asked.

'Not that I know of. Nor has there been a tornado in Delmere – or anywhere else in the county, if

I think about it,' said Dad. 'I'll send your mum a text as I'm sure she'll want to know about this.'

'Do you think there'll be anything on the news about it?' I asked.

'I doubt it'll make the national news, seeing as it's a local weather event. Though I'm looking at the *Thirkshire Herald* website right now and I can't see any mention of this tornado,' said Dad, scrolling through his phone. 'So maybe it wasn't that bad.'

'I want to see a tornado. Do you think there will be another one, Daddy?' asked Oscar.

'Trust me, Oscar, I don't think you'd want to see a tornado. They can be quite destructive, so let's just hope there won't be another one.'

'Yeah, we wouldn't want that, especially when we had our own tornado in this house on Saturday making a huge mess!' I said, looking daggers at Oscar and Ramona.

'And there'll be no repeat of that this evening,' Dad warned, throwing us a serious look. 'I want you *all* to behave when Mrs Armstrong's here, you got that?'

'Don't worry, Dad, we'll be on our very best behaviour,' I said, knowing how important it was that I won back his trust, especially if I wanted to see my pocket money again, and finally get a chance to tell him I have superpowers and have him believe me.

CHAPTER 21

At school, I tried my best not to think about my powers. I told Elliot about my plan of not using them for a while and I was surprised to see that he was a little upset about it.

'So does this mean I can't go flying again?' he groaned as we strolled around the playground during break.

'Afraid so, but it'll just be until my superpowers sort themselves out. Anyway, as I said, I'm going to give it a few days, then I'll try my powers out again.'

'Do you think that stuck place you found yourself in was real?' asked Elliot.

'It certainly felt real.'

'So you don't think it could've been a dream then, or halfway between a dream and reality?'

'Oh, we're not talking about dreams again, are we?! You've already seen my superpowers with your own eyes, so why do you still insist that I'm dreaming?'

Elliot shrugged. 'I don't mean to. I'm still trying to get used to the idea of you even having superpowers. I mean, I've known you for most of my life, and for all that time you could've had these abilities and didn't even know,' said Elliot, his face looking amazed all over again.

'I get what you're saying. It's been a lot for me too, trying to get my head around it all.'

'You probably don't even realise, Sonny, the extent of the things you could do with your powers, and I'm not just talking superhero stuff.'

'Like what?'

'Like breaking the world high jump record! Which you'd be able to do without even having to properly try.'

'Oh yeah. I hadn't thought of that. I really could break the world record if I wanted to!'

'So why don't you? You could do it today!' said Elliot.

'But wouldn't that be cheating, considering I'd be using my powers to do it?'

'I suppose … but I can just imagine the look on Parvin and Zeki's faces if they saw you do it.'

'Well, seeing as I don't want everyone knowing about my powers, there's no way I'm letting those two donuts see me break the world record, even if it did mean them never being able to diss my high-jumping skills again.'

Even though I hadn't planned to use my powers again for a while, I couldn't help but use them when I saw Delilah carrying a pile of books from the school library which looked like they were about to fall. With my mind, I quickly and discreetly adjusted the books so they didn't drop, and that sort of put me in a good mood. It was nice being able to use my powers to do something good for someone, and so I decided to perform a few more acts of kindness. It might've been pretty basic, but I used my powers to tie a rubbish bag that Mr Pearson had taken out of one of the bins in the corridor. I did it while he'd briefly stopped to talk to Mrs Banerjee, and when he looked back at the bag, Mr Pearson seemed both surprised and confused. But then he just shrugged and went on his way.

In my maths lesson, I used my powers to stop the clock on the wall during a test to give everyone an extra two minutes. Thankfully, Miss Kerrigan didn't notice. In PE, when we were playing basketball and Liam was trying to make a free throw, I gave the ball a little push with my mind so it'd drop through the hoop. I'd never seen Liam look so thrilled. And lastly, during afternoon break, when me and Elliot had gone to our school playing field, I used my telekinetic powers to open Elliot's packet of crisps and turn the pages of my X-Men comic that we were reading together. And of course Elliot was super pleased.

I decided I was going to tell Dad about my superpowers when he got home from work. Then once I'd told him, I'd tell Mum. But when I got in from school, Ramona and Oscar were home with Mrs Armstrong and Dad had already left to start his food delivery shift.

'Did you have a good day?' Mrs Armstrong asked me as I wandered into the kitchen, unsurprised to see that she was making her beloved chicken stew.

'Yeah, it was OK,' I answered before grabbing a banana and going up to my room to make a start on my homework.

I had geography and English homework to do tonight, and because I wanted to get it done quickly so I could play on my console, I used my powers to make my pen write everything out. I'm sure if kids at my school knew I had powers they'd be well jealous. I mean, who wouldn't want to be able to finish their homework in record time? And once I'd managed to collect an additional 500 stars playing *Star Stacks*, it was time for dinner.

As usual, I made sure to mix a good dose of ketchup into Mrs Armstrong's stew, not that she looked very pleased about it, the wrinkles in her face tightening with disapproval.

Ramona, on the other hand, was happily tucking in. As it happens, Mrs Armstrong's stew is one of the few things Ramona *doesn't* moan about.

'Your stew tastes extra delicious today, Mrs Armstrong,' she burbled, but it felt more like a dig aimed at me because she knew how bored I was of eating it.

'Why, thank you, Ramona!' said Mrs Armstrong, her wrinkles now crinkling with gratitude. 'Eat up, Oscar,' she ordered my brother, who was playing with his food as he often likes to do.

Oscar's not a fan of her stew either, but he does normally get round to finishing his plate.

After dinner, I returned to my room, as I didn't fancy watching the news with Mrs Armstrong. I played another one of my video games, one where I had to get my space-ship from one end of the galaxy to the other while avoiding being annihilated by giant asteroids and alien spacecraft. After that, I stared out of my telescope for a bit, and tonight there were lots of stars lining the black, velvety sky, including my favourite, Polaris, the North Star.

It was around nine thirty when I floated downstairs (well, it beat having to walk down them) to get myself a glass of milk. Dad still wasn't home yet, but I was determined to wait up so I could tell him about my powers. Just as I was pouring out my milk, the doorbell rang. Mrs Armstrong went and answered it while I peered into the hall. To my surprise, two police officers walked in, and from the look on their faces, I knew something bad had happened.

CHAPTER 22

My heart was beating so fast, it felt like it was going to beat right out of my chest at the sight of a policewoman and a policeman standing in the living room.

The policeman looked at me, and then looked at Mrs Armstrong.

'Could we talk in private?' he asked her. It was obvious he didn't want me to hear what they were going to say.

Mrs Armstrong glanced at me. 'Oh, don't worry about young Sonny here, he's just about to go to bed.'

'No! I want to know what's going on,' I said quickly. 'Why are you here? What's happened?'

The policeman looked unsurely at the policewoman, who gave a small shrug. He then looked back at me and nodded slowly.

'Could we sit down?' he asked, directing his question at Mrs Armstrong.

'Yes, sure,' Mrs Armstrong replied, and I could hear the worry in her voice, her hands trembling ever so slightly.

I tried to think of why they were here.

Did someone see me use my powers to lift the cars? Were they here to arrest me for causing all that damage?

My legs began to shake with fear, so I had to sit down as well.

'I'm PC Jasmine Bailey, and this is my colleague, PC Tom McGuigan,' the policewoman said to me.

'You know, I have a niece called Jasmine,' said Mrs Armstrong, trying to make her voice sound light and airy, only it came out in a wobble.

She seemed as scared as I was, for some reason, but it wasn't as if she was the one in big trouble.

'We really would like to speak to Mrs Lawson,' said PC McGuigan.

'She's working abroad,' said Mrs Armstrong. 'She works in the film industry and she's working on a film as we speak. But whatever you want to tell her, I can pass on the message.'

'Well, it's regarding Mr Lawson. He's the reason why we're here,' said PC Bailey, then paused for a moment that felt like the full length of a day, which made me feel doubly frightened.

'I'm afraid there was an accident, a collision involving Mr Lawson's bike and a car. Mr Lawson was subsequently taken to the hospital and his condition does appear to be very serious.'

'Oh my God!' a voice murmured, but I couldn't quite tell if it was me or Mrs Armstrong.

In less than a minute, PC Bailey's words felt like they'd completely changed my life, even more so than my superpowers.

'Do you think there's any way you could get hold of Mrs Lawson tonight?' asked PC Bailey.

'Um, yes. I'll see what I can do,' said Mrs Armstrong. Her voice sounded far away, even though she was only sitting inches from me.

After that, everything PC Bailey said felt like Milo Allerton's chewing-gum missiles firing their way towards me. Except her missiles were causing me serious pain in the pit of my stomach.

'The accident was on Chalingsford Lane.' 'We're still trying to establish how the collision happened.' 'Mr Lawson is unconscious.'

The room felt like it was spinning. If my dad was unconscious, then he might never wake up! I'd never felt more terrified in my whole life. I so badly wanted my mum, and was prepared to teleport myself to Jordan right there and then to bring her home. There was just one problem: I could barely move. It was as if I were sitting on a huge mound of chewing gum that was keeping me stuck to the chair.

So much for me having superpowers! I thought. What use were they when I couldn't even stand?

I suddenly wished I could go back just a few hours, when my world was still normal-*ish* and hadn't been turned on its axis by these two police officers with their grim faces. I would've given anything to have gone back to when we were sat in the conservatory eating Mrs Armstrong's stew. But unfortunately, I didn't have the type of superpower that could make me travel back in time.

CHAPTER 23

'My dad is still alive though, isn't he?' I blurted at PC Bailey, my voice so high and so piercing, it hurt my ears.

I didn't wait for her to answer as I said, 'I need to see him,' and my body finally found a way to move as I stood up, although my legs did feel a little unsteady and I almost fell back down into the chair.

'I think we need to get hold of your mother first,' said Mrs Armstrong.

'But she's in Jordan … We need to get to the hospital now!' I replied desperately.

Everything after that was a blur. The police officers left, and I think Mrs Armstrong made some tea because there'd be no way of explaining how I had a steaming cup of peppermint tea on a tray on my lap unless Mrs Armstrong had acquired some special powers of her own. I hadn't even drunk my glass of milk, which now felt like a lifetime ago since I'd poured it out before that dreaded sound of the doorbell.

'I called your mum's mobile but she's not picking up. I've left her a message.' Mrs Armstrong's voice began to fade in and out. 'But I think I know what to do. I'll call Eunice and ask her to come over, so there's someone here in case Ramona and Oscar wake up. You and I can go to the hospital.'

I nodded and put down the tray without having had a single sip of the tea. At some point, Mrs Okaru came to the house. It could've only been five or ten minutes later, but it was as if time had become all confusing, just like when I'd been in The Stuck Place. The next thing I knew, Mrs Armstrong and I were in the back of a minicab on our way to the hospital.

The whole journey felt mega slow, even though the roads were really quiet. The minicab driver had the radio playing. It was one of those stations that my mum and dad liked to listen to that play mushy love songs twenty-four-seven. The music just added to my restlessness. I urgently needed to see my dad, and if I could have, I would've just lifted the car and whizzed us off to the hospital. But my mind was like a traffic jam of so many thoughts, so there was no way I could've got it to focus and lift the cab.

When we finally reached the hospital, I jumped straight out of the cab and ran through the car park to the hospital's entrance, Mrs Armstrong hurrying behind.

'Slow down, Sonny! I'm an old woman, I can't run as fast as you,' she called.

When we got inside, Mrs Armstrong told me to sit in the waiting area while she went to the A&E reception desk to ask about Dad. She had to wait in a queue, and I found myself feeling really frustrated because I couldn't take all this waiting any longer! I just wanted to see my dad! I *had* to know if he was going to be all right.

'They don't seem to want to tell me much,' said Mrs Armstrong when she joined me in the waiting area. 'I think it's because I'm not a family member, though I did manage to get a bit more detail,' she whispered as she sat down beside me. 'It sounds like they're performing emergency surgery on Adam.'

My heart rattled in my ribcage.

'Now, now, Sonny, please try not to worry,' said Mrs Armstrong as I looked at her with an anxious face. 'I'm sure the doctors are doing all they can.'

She squeezed my shoulder as I stared gloomily at the floor.

Dad will be OK, I told myself, trying to drown out a

taunting voice in my head that was saying my dad wasn't going to make it. And as this internal voice battle kicked off, it was the negative one that grew louder and louder, and I was desperate to make it stop.

'I've got superpowers!' I blurted aloud, which immediately silenced the negative voice.

'You've got what, dear?' said Mrs Armstrong, looking at me curiously.

'Superpowers,' I repeated, but in an almost defeated way, because right now I sure didn't feel like I had any powers. I'd never felt so weak and helpless. I was silly to think I could ever be a superhero.

'That's interesting,' Mrs Armstrong said blandly.

'I'm not lying when I say that.'

'No, I believe you,' she answered, but it was quite obvious from the look on her face that she didn't.

'I can move things with my mind, and I can fly and teleport. Only, I can't get my powers to work at the moment,' I told her, as I fought back the tears that began to well in my eyes. 'Don't cry,' I found myself saying out loud, but I hadn't meant to.

Mrs Armstrong squeezed my shoulder again.

'If you want to cry, Sonny, you go ahead and cry,' she whispered.

'But I have to be strong for Dad and my mum, and Ramona and Oscar …' I put my head in my hands.

'I understand you might feel like that, but being strong isn't about pushing your emotions to one side, especially when something so upsetting has happened,' said Mrs Armstrong, and she began to cry. Luckily I had a tissue in my pocket.

'Thank you, Sonny,' she whispered.

We carried on waiting, and soon an hour went by, but we still had no news on Dad, and the waiting was becoming unbearable! I dozed off for a while, but when Mrs Armstrong woke me up, we were *still* waiting.

'Sonny, I need to get you home, it's very late and you do have school in the morning,' she said to me as she got up from the chair.

'We can't go! We have to make sure my dad's going to be all right,' I said pleadingly, tugging at her cardigan sleeve, like I was hanging off a cliff and Mrs Armstrong was the only one who could bring me back up to safety. That was certainly how I felt.

'It's unlikely we're going to get any more news tonight, Sonny,' said Mrs Armstrong. 'I've already ordered a minicab. It'll be here soon.'

My heart sank to my feet. Well, that's where it felt like it had landed, and I even imagined it lying beside me looking all squidgy and hopeless before getting swept away by the cleaner who was mopping the floor.

Our journey home felt just as agonising as our journey to the hospital.

'You mustn't worry about your dad, Sonny, he'll be OK, he's in good hands,' said Mrs Okaru when Mrs Armstrong and I got back to the house.

But as I made my way to bed, one thought just kept circling my brain.

Was my dad going to live or was he going to die?

CHAPTER 24

The next day I was woken up by Oscar, who jumped on to my bed, wanting to know where Dad was.

'Mrs Armstrong won't tell us. Did he go to work early?' he asked.

I so wanted last night to have been an awful dream, but seeing the look of concern on Oscar's face was a reminder that it hadn't been.

Should I tell my brother that Dad was in hospital?

'Where is Daddy? Tell me!' said Oscar.

'You're right. He's working an early shift,' I mumbled. 'Lots of people need their takeaway breakfast, Osc,' I added as he flounced off my bed.

'I want Daddy here to get *my* breakfast. I don't want Mrs Armstrong making it,' Oscar complained.

'It's only Rice Krispies and milk. You could make it yourself.'

He sighed. 'I know, but Daddy's way of making it is the best.'

When I came downstairs Mrs Armstrong was pottering about in the living room nervously.

'Your brother and sister were asking where your dad is, but I couldn't think of anything to say,' she said quietly.

'Don't worry, I told Oscar that he's gone to work.'

Mrs Armstrong nodded. 'Maybe we should just try and keep everything normal. I'll take them to school, and you'll need to get off to school as well.'

'But I want to go to the hospital.'

'No, Sonny, I can't let you miss school.' She looked at me sympathetically. 'Look, I left my number with the hospital so if I hear anything I promise I'll text you. I've also left your mother some more messages, so hopefully she'll give me a call soon.'

'I wish she was here,' I muttered solemnly.

When I met up with Elliot at the bus stop, I told him about last night, and I'd never seen him look so worried for me. I found it quite hard telling him about the accident, and my voice went all croaky with tears, so I had to keep taking these big gulps to force the tears back down.

'It's so annoying that I can't go and see my dad at the hospital,' I told him.

'But you could if you teleported there,' said Elliot.

It was a sensible suggestion, and had it not been for the negative voice inside my head, I would've teleported myself to the hospital right away and wouldn't have cared if hundreds of people saw that I have superpowers. Only, the voice was telling me not to go and was making me think that if I went, I'd be sure to get bad news.

My emotions were feeling really jumbled and confused because, on the one hand, I was desperate to see my dad, but on the other, I just wanted to block everything out and not even think about what had happened. And because I was so frightened of the possibility of receiving bad news, I switched off my phone rather than keep it on mute like I normally do when I'm at school. I just couldn't run the risk of getting a text from Mrs Armstrong telling me the worst.

'I would teleport myself there, but my powers are still misbehaving,' I told Elliot, which wasn't exactly a lie, considering I was still trying to figure out how to make my powers work correctly *all* of the time.

'Well, try not to worry, Sonny, I'm sure your dad will be OK,' said Elliot, just like Mrs Armstrong and Mrs Okaru had said.

I know they were all trying to be kind and trying to

put my mind at ease by making out Dad would be fine, but how could any of them know this was true, when (a) none of them were doctors; and (b) none of them had superpowers like me? In their case, though, they would have needed psychic powers to see into the future to know that.

CHAPTER 25

Getting through the first half of the day felt particularly difficult, and it wasn't because of the insanely hard equations I had to solve during maths, or because Milo Allerton threw me a dirty look when I passed him in the corridor, or even because I got asked up to the board again. This time it was during science, my favourite subject. I failed to correctly identify the vacuole in a picture of a cell. None of that was as tough as trying to deal with my worry about Dad. I also felt like I had a porcupine living in my stomach, because I just had this constant prickly ache.

But I did manage to get a little relief during history, following an earful Mr Goodwin had given to the whole class after Parvin and Zeki, who'd been flicking elastic bands at each other, flicked one of the bands at Mr Goodwin's nose. He told us that we were the worst Year Sevens he'd ever taught and that, as far as he could see, we were not the least bit interested in history.

His ranting and raving were seriously getting on my nerves, so I decided to really give Mr Goodwin something to complain about. As my brain began to buzz, with my powers I snatched the whiteboard pen he was holding, though to Mr Goodwin and everyone else it just looked like he'd dropped it.

As Mr Goodwin went to pick up the pen, I made it roll away, then stop. When he reached out for the pen, I made it roll and then stop again. When Mr Goodwin went to grab the pen a third time, I made it roll some more. A few kids laughed as Mr Goodwin took a creeping step forward as if to catch the pen unawares, but when he quickly tried to seize hold of it, the pen continued to roll away from him. It wasn't long before Mr Goodwin was chasing the pen around the room, with the whole class in complete hysterics.

'Are you doing that?' whispered Elliot to me.

I grinned at him, which made Elliot grin too.

'Maybe the pen's possessed, sir,' said Parvin, trying to contain his laughter as Mr Goodwin scrambled past his table in hot pursuit.

'Trying to be the class comedian really doesn't suit

you, Parvin,' Mr Goodwin grumbled, going red in the face. Yet he seemed determined not to give up trying to get the pen.

'I think it's Mr Goodwin who's possessed,' I heard Holly whisper to Delilah with a giggle. 'It's just a stupid pen.'

But it was as if Mr Goodwin had something to prove, and it felt like he cared as much about a silly blue marker as he did about history. And with each new lap that Mr Goodwin made around the room, our laughter only grew, until we were literally wheezing, just like Mr Goodwin, who, after looking like he'd run a marathon, finally decided to give up. He returned to his desk, slumping down in his chair in exhaustion.

Finally I made the pen roll right back to him. But he no longer seemed interested and even kicked the pen away.

All the hoo-ha had managed to take some of my worries away, and at the same time helped to turn down that negative voice inside my head until it was just a tiny squeak, as a much more positive and cheerier voice boomed over it. The positive voice was telling me that Dad's emergency surgery had gone very well and that he was probably sitting up in bed waiting to see some visitors. I still didn't feel courageous enough to switch on my phone, though, as the squeaky negative voice kept squeaking at me not to.

CHAPTER 26

I had high jump practice after school and today I was struggling to clear 1.24m, even though I'd cleared it loads of times before. My heart just wasn't in it.

Elliot managed to clear both 1.24m and 1.26m and his body just about made it over the bar at 1.28m, while Liam managed to clear 1.30m and 1.40m, all of which he's never done before. This made both my and Elliot's eyes literally POP OUT of our heads, because we just couldn't believe it! Then I almost CHOKED on the water I was drinking at the sight of Liam comfortably clearing 1.50m, and I swear both Elliot and I almost COLLAPSED in shock when Liam went straight over the bar at 1.60m. It was incredible because Liam was normally worse than me and Elliot! Before this, he could just about get over 1.20m.

'Since when have you been able to jump that high?' I asked Liam, barely able to get my words out because I was just so shocked.

'I guess I'm just getting better at it,' he replied with a shrug as Parvin came over.

'But nobody becomes that good that fast,' said Elliot. 'At our last practice session, you refused to go over the bar when it was moved to one twenty-two. And now a week later you're asking for the bar to be moved up to one sixty! Just how is that possible?'

'I've improved my technique, what can I say? But if you really must know, the reason why I was passing on those heights was that I just didn't feel ready to attempt them. I guess I didn't realise I had the ability all along to jump as high as one sixty.'

'And you just suddenly realised this today?!' I said.

'Don't listen to him, Liam, he's just jealous,' said Parvin as he shook Liam's hand. 'Welcome to the winners' club, my friend! You're officially no longer a loser. Plus, you might just have what it takes to be a high jump champion.'

'Thanks,' said Liam, grinning from ear to ear as he and Parvin strolled off together.

'So, all this time, he was hiding how good he was,' said Elliot, shaking his head.

'Well, as the saying goes: nothing ventured, nothing gained,' I replied.

It was something my dad liked to say sometimes, but thinking of him only made my stomach ache again.

'Well, the risk he took certainly paid off, and now he stands a much better chance than me of getting selected to compete in the county championship in July,' said Elliot. Then, noticing a changed look on my face, he asked, 'Are you all right, Sonny?'

'D'you know what? I don't even know why I'm acting as if I couldn't clear one sixty when I've got superpowers. I'm sure I could clear it no problem.'

'You could break the world record,' Elliot hinted again. 'I reckon you could jump higher than three metres!'

'No one in the world has ever cleared three metres, but actually, I think I could clear five or even fifteen metres!'

'Why not do it then?' Elliot urged. 'It won't be official or anything, but at least you'll know you've broken the world record.'

I started to nod. 'I might just,' I mulled, as an exciting feeling ran through me, which was enough to keep my worried feelings at bay, for a short while at least. 'Do you know what? I will do it!' I declared.

CHAPTER 27

'Come on, you two, hurry up,' Mr Jarvis called to me and Elliot at the end of our athletics practice as kids began to head back to the changing rooms.

'Coming, sir. I'm just doing up my laces,' said Elliot, as Mr Jarvis rolled his eyes.

He went back inside with the others, leaving just me and Elliot on the school field. So with nobody else around, I now had the chance to break the world record.

The bar was still at 1.60m from when Liam had done his jump, and with the buzzing sound now in my head, I used my telekinetic powers to lift the bar until it was set to three metres.

Elliot and I gave each other a high-five and then I got into position, ready to take a running jump – or should I say a flying jump, because I made myself soar to a height where I was almost touching the clouds, the world beneath me feeling vast, but at the same time everything becoming miniature, including the houses and my school, which looked like a tiny matchbox. As I arched my back, coming back down was even better, the wind pinching my cheeks as I glided downwards, and when I landed on the mat, I couldn't have felt happier.

'So do you think I broke the world record?' I said to Elliot, even though I knew I had.

'You didn't just break the record, Sonny, you smashed it to SMITHEREENS! And I don't think there'll ever be anyone who breaks your record.'

'I really did just go and break the world record, didn't I?!' I said, looking around our school field, imagining it was a stadium packed with people clapping and cheering. I imagined Dad was there too, cheering the loudest. Then I gave a little sigh. 'Technically, I did cheat,' I said to Elliot. 'My superpowers do give me a very unfair advantage.'

Still, I made my way home with a big smile on my face. But when I reached the top of my road my worry completely broke free and I felt like I couldn't breathe.

What if Dad's dead? were the horrible words that surged through my mind again.

I didn't want to go home. I didn't want Mrs Armstrong to give me that news, and I didn't want to see my brother and sister's bleak faces, because it would break me. I had to get as far away from my street as possible. As my body began to tingle, I teleported to the first place I could think of.

'What the … ?! Where did you spring from?!' said a startled voice.

I was in Ice To Meet You, and it was Mr Buckley whom I'd frightened.

'I didn't see you come in,' he said, looking at me from the counter as I sat in one of the booths.

For a second I wondered if he thought there was something suspicious about me.

'You probably didn't see me because I, erm … went straight to the toilet when I came in. I was bursting.'

'Oh … right,' Mr Buckley said slowly. 'So are you going to order something?' he asked in a frank tone.

I approached the counter and ordered a cookie-dough ice cream. I was relieved I didn't teleport to The Stuck Place, and hoped my time there had been a one-off blip.

I knew Mrs Armstrong would be wondering where I was, but I found myself ordering another cup of ice cream, then another and another, because I just wasn't ready to go home. I guess in a way I was trying to psych myself up in case … you know. Yet devouring several cups of cookie-dough ice cream didn't make me feel any braver. It was getting late, and soon I was the only person left in the ice-cream parlour. Delilah was helping her dad to clear up and came over to me.

'I don't want to rush you, but it's almost eight o'clock and we'll be closing in a minute.'

I nodded.

'Did you have high jump practice this afternoon?' she asked.

'Yup.'

'Break any records?' she said, even though it's common knowledge that I'm rubbish at the high jump.

'Yes, I broke the world record actually,' I said, and I don't know why but there was a part of me that felt like telling Delilah about my powers. Her face of course was completely disbelieving, so I quickly said, 'Only joking. I wish I *could* break the world record. Maybe one day.'

I pulled my phone out of my rucksack and stared at it for a minute trying to decide whether to switch it on. No doubt I had loads of messages from Mrs Armstrong wanting to know where I was. I expect she'd give me a telling-off when I got in, which made me smile because that was something I could handle very easily, and I hoped that was all I had to face. I quickly shoved my phone back into my rucksack and slung it over my shoulder, deciding that I'd wait until I got home to deal with whatever Mrs Armstrong was going to say to me.

'I'll see you,' I called to Delilah, but when I turned back round she was no longer at the counter.

I went over to it and noticed there was a small teddy bear, which hadn't been there earlier. I picked it up and looked into its brown eyes, which glistened under the light. Maybe a little kid had forgotten it. I put it back down and headed for the door.

'Bye, Sonny,' trilled Delilah, making me jump, and I turned back round.

'That's weird, you weren't there a second ago,' I said to her.

'I was out the back, helping my dad put out the rubbish,' she said, giving me a smile that could power a thousand light bulbs, and my hands started to fizz.

Her smile was so pretty, and for an awkward moment I couldn't think of anything to say, before I spotted that the teddy was no longer on top of the counter.

'I think someone left their—'

'Teddy, yeah someone did,' Delilah replied. 'I've just put it in a drawer underneath. They'll probably come back for it at some point.'

'OK, well, I'll see you at school tomorrow,' I said.

'Yep, see you tomorrow,' she responded.

As I stepped out of Ice To Meet You, I still wasn't ready to go home, so I decided to teleport somewhere else, somewhere that I hoped would cheer me up, seeing as the ice cream I'd eaten hadn't managed to do that. In my head, I pictured where I wanted to go, and as my arms and legs began to tingle, I immediately appeared in my favourite place – the planetarium.

I always enjoyed visiting the planetarium, which was in Ocean View, and right now what made it even better was that there wasn't anyone else around. I was the only person in the whole planetarium! Well, it was past closing time. I was in a room which had an exhibit dedicated to the solar system. This exhibit was my favourite, as it had these giant 3D models of the planets hanging down from the ceiling, their fluorescent glow making them look spectacular in the dark. I focused my mind on them excitedly, and as my brain began to buzz, I made the planets spin.

Around the room were stands with smaller models of each planet. I made all of them come towards me: Earth, Mercury, Venus, Mars, Saturn, Uranus, Neptune and Jupiter – which happens to be the planet I love the most. I then made them whirr around me. It was awesome!

Suddenly I could hear the sound of footsteps and keys jangling. I stopped focusing on the little planets moving around me and they all fell noisily to the floor. Straight away the footsteps and the sound of the keys became louder. I felt like I was back in Mr Pearson's storeroom, about to get into serious trouble. I had to get away, so I thought of home. As a tingly feeling rushed through me, within a short moment I was standing outside my front door. I took a minute, staring at it anxiously before turning the key.

'Oh, thank God!' said a voice, but it wasn't Mrs Armstrong.

'Mum!' I gasped as I stepped inside the house.

Only, the person who came running towards me and held me in their arms wasn't my mum.

'I'm here to take care of you, Sonny, and everything's going to be all right,' said my Auntie Cleo.

And it was at that precise moment I started to cry these big raindrop-sized tears; tears I'd been holding in since Dad's accident, which wouldn't stop flowing.

CHAPTER 28

It was a shock seeing my Auntie Cleo because I hadn't seen her since I was five, and I'd also forgotten how much she looked like Mum (well, an older version of her) and how much she sounded like her too.

'We were about to organise a search party to come and look for you,' she said, as I ate a toasted ham-and-ketchup sandwich that she'd made for me after I'd eventually stopped crying.

'Yes, both me and your aunt have been calling and texting you all evening, Sonny,' said Mrs Armstrong. 'I know you have high jump practice on a Wednesday, but you should've been back hours ago. Cleo and I were really worried.'

Auntie Cleo sat down next to me. 'You really should

keep your phone switched on.' She was even nagging me like Mum.

'How come you're here? Where's my mum?' I asked her.

'She's still in Jordan, Sonny, but she'll be back soon. She's hoping to fly home on Sunday, so in the meantime she's asked me to stay and look after you all.'

Auntie Cleo was practically a stranger, so it seemed odd that Mum would want her looking after us, especially as she still wanted to put some space between them. Anyway, I didn't need her looking after me. I could look after myself. I was almost a teenager, after all.

'Why would my mum want you looking after us?' I said to her questioningly.

'I expect it's probably come as a surprise, seeing as you haven't seen me in years,' said Auntie Cleo, as if she could read my thoughts. 'You were all so much younger the last time I saw you. Oscar was just a baby.' She smiled. 'However, me and your mum have managed to resolve our differences and it's times like this when people need to have their family around.'

'Yeah, I need my mum! Why couldn't she just come back today?' I replied crossly.

'Well, I'm sure she would've loved to have jumped on a plane straight away,' said Auntie Cleo, clearing her throat awkwardly. 'But I think it's a case of Beverley needing to make sure her team of make-up artists can cope without her.'

'I want to speak to my mum.'

'She's promised to call tomorrow.'

'And I want my dad ...' My voice broke off. 'He will be OK, won't he?'

I looked at Auntie Cleo furtively, as a sea of emotions began to swish and swirl inside me again. Her face became grave, as did Mrs Armstrong's.

'There's no easy way of saying this, Sonny, but I'm afraid your dad is in a coma,' said Auntie Cleo, putting her arm around me. 'The doctors did manage to stop the internal bleeding he had, but he's still very unwell.'

Just like last night, my heart felt like it had fallen out of my chest, but this time it was as if it had tumbled into my stomach and was squishing down on the ham-and-ketchup sandwich and all the ice cream that I'd eaten. And now I felt like I was going to puke.

'But he will wake up, won't he?' I said, rubbing my belly to prevent a projectile spew.

'We're praying that he does,' said Auntie Cleo.

'But you don't even like my dad,' I murmured, as a memory of the last time Auntie Cleo was here flicked through my mind.

'I know your dad and I haven't always seen eye to

eye, but I do want to put those disagreements that we had behind us.'

'Do Oscar and Ramona know about the accident?' I asked.

'Yes, I spoke to them before they went to bed, so they know. They were very upset, but like I said to them, I truly believe Adam will wake up from his coma and will be back home before you know it.'

'Can I see my dad tomorrow? *Please*,' I pleaded. 'I don't want to go to school. It was so hard today, and I was so scared.'

'Sure, I can take you to see your dad tomorrow. In fact, I'll take all of you,' said Auntie Cleo.

'And you needn't be scared, Sonny,' said Mrs Armstrong. 'I too believe your dad will pull through. Anyway, didn't you tell me you have superpowers?' She smiled gently. 'So how about you use them to drive that fear away?' she added, even though I knew she didn't believe for one second that I had powers.

'You have superpowers?' said Auntie Cleo, looking at me curiously.

'I was only kidding when I said that,' I quickly lied. Right now, that wasn't what I wanted to talk about. 'Superpowers aren't real, everyone knows that,' I said, trying to move the conversation on. 'So you promise, I can definitely see my dad tomorrow?'

'Yes, I promise, Sonny,' said Auntie Cleo. 'And it's important that you, me and everyone else stay positive, for your dad's sake at least.'

'I know,' I replied limply, as I repeated her words over and over in my head to push back all those negative thoughts trying to barrel their way to the front of my mind.

You have to stay positive, Sonny. You have to stay positive.

CHAPTER 29

I hadn't managed to sleep that much as I kept thinking about Dad being in a coma, and even though I was trying my best to stay positive, it wasn't proving easy. I knew Ramona and Oscar would be feeling upset, so I decided I'd make them breakfast, only Auntie Cleo beat me to it. She'd made each of us boiled egg and soldiers, which made me feel like a little kid. I'm too old to have my toast cut up for me! I couldn't help feeling annoyed. I wanted to have some Rice Krispies like normal, but when I went to the fridge to get the milk, it wasn't there.

I went into the living room, where Auntie Cleo was sitting on the floor surrounded by paperwork.

'Welcome to my life as a project manager,' she said as she looked up at me from her laptop. 'I hope you don't mind me turning the living room into my mini-office. I normally work from home.'

But I did mind.

'There's no more almond milk in the fridge,' I said.

'Oh, I'm sorry. I had the last of it in my tea, but I'll remember to buy some more when I go to the shops,' she said, getting up. 'Just to check, you can eat eggs, can't you?'

'Yeah,' I mumbled, following her as she went to the kitchen. 'We are still going to the hospital, aren't we?' I said, just to make sure.

'Yes, we'll go this morning,' said Auntie Cleo as she went over to one of the cupboards and looked through it. 'I must say, it was very interesting what Mrs Armstrong said last night about you telling her you had super-powers.'

'Like I said, I was just kidding,' I answered, sitting down at the kitchen table.

'It would be great to have superpowers, don't you think?' said Auntie Cleo, turning around as she held a packet of digestive biscuits.

I shrugged.

'For example, imagine having the strength to be able to lift anything,' she said.

'Yeah, I guess that would be cool,' I replied, dipping one of my toast soldiers into my egg.

But it wasn't as if I needed to be super strong to be able to lift things, seeing as I could just move them with my mind.

'You sound like you believe in superpowers,' I said, which made me wonder if it'd be easy to convince Auntie Cleo that I had powers.

'My dad used to say, never doubt the impossible, and I think he had a point,' she responded, munching on a digestive.

Oscar and Ramona came into the kitchen, and today they weren't their usual boisterous selves. Their faces were crestfallen.

'Just to let you know, kids, I'm going to take you to see your dad at the hospital, so you won't have to go to school today,' Auntie Cleo told them.

'Will Daddy be awake when we see him?' Oscar asked, looking at me.

'Probably not, but he will be waking up real soon, Oscar, you'll see,' I replied.

'And then he can come home, and we can have a party for him,' said Oscar.

'That's a cool idea,' I mused. 'I think Dad would like that.'

An hour later we were waiting for a minicab to come and take us to the hospital, and when it arrived, I quietly told Oscar that I'd buy him some sweets, which made his eyes light up. But once again, Auntie Cleo beat me to it. She just so happened to have some sweets in her handbag and was sharing them out in the cab. I was too annoyed with her to take any for myself.

'No, thank you,' I said in a gruff voice when she offered a sweet, and I didn't feel guilty seeing as she'd ruined my plan.

Auntie Cleo pretended not to notice my tone, and said, 'I'll save you a couple, in case you change your mind.'

During the journey, I thought about how I'd break it to Dad that I have superpowers when he eventually woke up. I considered making it like a surprise present for both him and my mum, and before you ask how superpowers can be turned into a present for someone: well, when my mum got pregnant with me, she made the pregnancy a surprise present for my dad. He's always said it was the best present he ever received, when really it was just a note in a gift box that said: *I'm pregnant!*

So maybe I could do the same: write a note that said *I have superpowers!* and put it in a box with a bow on top shaped like a star. I think my dad would like that.

CHAPTER 30

When we got to the hospital, we were directed to a ward where Dad had his own room, but the weird thing was, even though I'd been so eager to see him, seeing my dad looking so helpless made me just want to run away. He had cuts and bruises on his face and tubes were coming out of his nose and arms, and there was a heart monitor machine beside him. Oscar held on to Auntie Cleo's hand, not wanting to get too close to the bed. He was scared, just like me. He had with him one of his five Power Piglets, after saying earlier he was going to give it to Dad so he wouldn't be on his own. Ramona, however, went straight over to Dad and gently touched his forehead.

'Hi, Dad,' she said to him. 'I have a spelling test at

school tomorrow. I've been practising all the words like "appreciate", which is spelt *a-p-p-r-e-c-i-a-t-e*.'

Ramona was just talking to him like she normally does.

'I appreciate you, Dad, for all that you've done for us,' she said.

'Hey, Oscar, why don't you give your daddy your Power Piglet?' said Auntie Cleo.

He looked up at her uncertainly. 'Do you think he knows that we're here? Will he be able to hear me?'

'He might be able to, so go on, you can speak to him,' said Auntie Cleo encouragingly.

Oscar slowly walked towards the bed, and he was so much braver than me as I continued to hang back.

Oscar stared at Dad for a long moment before holding out his Power Piglet to him.

'This is for you, Daddy,' he said, as though Dad would wake up and take it from him. He then dropped his head sullenly like he realised this wasn't going to happen.

'We'll put it here,' said Auntie Cleo softly, taking the Power Piglet from him and placing it at the foot of Dad's bed. 'I'm sure your daddy will be very grateful you've given this to him.'

Auntie Cleo went and held Dad's hand. 'I hope you can hear me, Adam. I'm sorry we're having to meet under these circumstances after such a long time,' she said slowly. 'Your family miss you very much, so you get better soon, do you hear me? We want to hear those quirky phrases of yours like *fizzy lemons*, *sticky mayonnaise*, *sweaty salmon*. Those are a few I remember.'

'Actually, it's *sticky marmalade* and *smelly salmon*,' I corrected her, but I remained right where I was in the corner of the room.

'Oh, right,' Auntie Cleo mumbled, looking at me, then back at Dad. 'I guess we've got lots to catch up on.'

'We're going to have a party for you, Daddy, when you come home, and we're going to have lots of balloons and cake,' said Oscar.

'Did you hear that, Adam?' said Auntie Cleo. 'The children are going to throw you a big welcome home party.'

Ramona started crying.

'Oh, Ramona, don't cry,' said Auntie Cleo, giving her a hug.

I wish I could've comforted my sister. I wish there was a way my superpowers could've cheered us all up. But my powers just felt super pointless. I mean, it's not as if they could wake my dad up from his coma so everyone could be happy again.

Auntie Cleo turned to me. 'Why don't you come and have a chat with your dad?'

I shook my head.

'Surely you'd like to speak to him?'

I shrugged, but really I was just too afraid.

She came over to me. 'Look, I know you're probably feeling anxious about seeing him like this, and it's OK to feel like that,' Auntie Cleo whispered. 'I'll tell you what. Me, Ramona and Oscar will pop out the room so you can have some time with your dad, just you and him.'

She patted my shoulder.

'Come on, you two,' said Auntie Cleo to Ramona and Oscar. 'We're going to go and get some snacks while Sonny has a chat with your dad.'

Ramona and Oscar followed Auntie Cleo out while I continued to stand in the corner as though I were in trouble. After a few minutes, I slowly slunk over to the bed, sitting down on the easy chair. On the arm was a small box of tissues, and I took one out to distract myself, all the while not looking at Dad. I placed the tissue flat in my hand and as a buzzing sound echoed throughout my head, I telekinetically made the tissue fold once, twice, then three times before I made my powers unfold it so it was flat in my hand again.

I wish Dad could've woken up and seen my superpowers for himself.

I stared at the tissue again as my mind scrunched it up into a ball, then made it float off and zip around the room.

Hesitantly I looked over at Dad.

'We all need you to wake up,' I said. 'Everyone's so sad and I don't know what to do or what to say.'

My eyes went back to following the ball of tissue as it flew around the room. Then I directed it back to me and stuffed it into my pocket.

I slowly looked at Dad again, biting my lip as I tried to think of something else to say.

'I've got something *splendtaculous* to tell you, and I'm hoping you'll be impressed, only you have to wake up first,' I told him. 'Please wake up.' I paused for a minute. 'I want you to know that you're the best dad in the entire galaxy and you are going to wake up because … you have to. You just have to!'

CHAPTER 31

Later that day, Mum phoned. It was so good to hear her voice and I told her how much I couldn't wait for her to come home.

'The hospital has been keeping me up to date on how your dad's been doing, but I don't want you to worry, Sonny. I have every faith he'll come out of his coma,' said Mum, though her voice sounded incredibly sad.

'And you are definitely coming home?' I said. Then, checking Auntie Cleo was out of earshot, I whispered, 'Auntie Cleo is getting on my nerves.'

'Yes, I'll be back on Sunday, but, Sonny, I hope you're not being rude to your aunt.'

'I'm not, but she keeps doing things I wanted to do.

Like this morning, I wanted to make everyone breakfast, but she did it.'

'Well, I did ask your Auntie Cleo to come and look after you, so that's what she's doing, sweetheart.'

'I hardly know her though, and you don't even get on with her that much.'

'She's my sister, Sonny, and we're getting on a lot more now than we did a few years back. Plus, I needed someone I could rely on to take care of you all.'

'You could've asked Mrs Armstrong to look after us.'

'But she's not family,' said Mum. 'Look, even though me and your aunt had a big falling-out, which thankfully is all in the past, deep down she is very kind and caring. She will take great care of you, so I want you to be good, do you understand?'

'Yeah, I understand.' I sighed.

Still, Auntie Cleo continued to annoy me, first by watering our plants and putting out the rubbish, which are usually my chores, and I'm sure Dad would've wanted me keeping up with them. And even when I told Auntie Cleo that I was happy to do it all, she wouldn't let me.

'I'm here to help, Sonny, so you just leave all the household work to me,' she said.

And that evening I wanted to make us all a special dinner. Well, I wasn't too bothered about Auntie Cleo, but I wanted to do it for Ramona and Oscar. And if I'm ever going to be a superhero for the neighbourhood – and maybe one day the world – then I need to start by being a hero for my family. Ramona and Oscar seemed happy enough when I told them what I planned to cook, except Auntie Cleo decided to go one better by saying she'd take us out for dinner.

'I can't possibly expect you to cook, Sonny – plus, I think you all deserve a treat,' she said.

And of course, Ramona and Oscar didn't say no. My sausages and beans were never going to compete with a tasty pizza from Big Sal's. It should've been me treating my brother and sister, not Auntie Cleo! It was like she was muscling in on my territory.

I was starting to understand why my dad didn't like her. She was super annoying, and I most *definitely* didn't like Auntie Cleo either!

CHAPTER 32

We got the bus to Big Sal's, and on our way there, Auntie Cleo said she wanted to know more about us and asked us to tell her some of our likes and dislikes. Oscar told her that he didn't like broccoli or beetroot or almond milk (not that he should even be drinking my almond milk). Then he told her about his love of the Power Piglets.

Ramona, on the other hand, just chose to tell Auntie Cleo all her dislikes, going on a right moan-fest about how she hates it when she thinks me and Oscar aren't listening to her, and how she dislikes having to wait for her turn to use the bathroom every morning. She didn't like a girl in her class called Flora because she was her main rival when it came to being top of the class in spelling. She also didn't like prawn cocktail crisps, squirrels and the deputy head teacher at her school, Mrs Mahoney, whom the kids have nicknamed Moody Mahoney.

'You don't like cute little squirrels?' said Auntie Cleo, very surprised.

Ramona shook her head. 'It's their tails, it's just so … *eeuw*!'

When Auntie Cleo asked to hear my likes and dislikes, I decided to say very little.

'I like ketchup,' I said, keeping it brief.

'Is that it?' said Auntie Cleo. 'I'm sure I remember you liking anything to do with space.'

'Yeah, I still do,' I mumbled.

'And your mum tells me you're on your school's athletics team and you do the high jump. So I assume that's something else you enjoy.'

'It's all right, I guess.'

'Okey-dokey, so what are your dislikes?'

I wanted to tell Auntie Cleo that I disliked her, but instead I said dairy because of my allergy. It brings me out in rashes. I was also quiet in the restaurant because I really didn't fancy making any small talk with her.

'Wow, will you look at this!' said Auntie Cleo, reading the menu. 'They do a grape and sardine pizza. I don't think I've ever heard of a more bizarre topping. I think I'll stay well clear in case it gives me a dodgy stomach!'

She laughed, and so did Ramona and Oscar, but I didn't, keeping my eyes locked on the menu.

'I think I'll just settle for a Hawaiian pizza,' Auntie Cleo decided.

'Me too,' chirped Ramona.

'You don't like Hawaiian pizza. You hate pineapples,' I sniffed at my sister.

'I don't *hate* pineapples. I just sometimes don't like to eat them. Anyway, I want to have what Auntie Cleo's having,' said Ramona as I scowled at her.

'Sonny, do you know what you'd like to have?' asked Auntie Cleo.

'I'll just have a cheese pizza.'

'That's a bit plain,' she replied.

'Well, it's my favourite.'

'You've always said pepperoni is your favourite,' said Oscar, landing me in it.

'It *used* to be my favourite,' I pointed out, as Auntie Cleo looked at me with a raised eyebrow. 'But *plain* cheese pizzas are now my favourite.'

'Don't worry, it's fine if you want to order that,' said Auntie Cleo.

She waved at a waiter, who was just finishing taking the orders at another table, and he came over.

'Oscar, do you want to tell this gentleman what you'd like?' said Auntie Cleo to my brother.

'Pepperoni!' he said, throwing his arm up as if he'd won a medal or something.

The waiter looked at me next.

'I'll have the individual soya cheese pizza, please.'

'And me and my niece will have the Hawaiian pizza,' said Auntie Cleo.

When our pizzas arrived, the topic of conversation shifted to what we all wanted to be when we grow up.

I told Auntie Cleo I wasn't sure what I wanted to be, just to be difficult. But really, I'd like to become an astrophysicist. Moaner (I was back to calling her that) said she wanted to become an author, and Oscar said he wanted to be a 'famous actor just like Dad', which for some reason made Auntie Cleo wince.

'That's a very tough profession, Oscar, which your dad was obviously struggling to succeed in,' she said. 'Which is why he was riding around on a bicycle delivering food. I'm sure he and your mum wish he *was* famous. And perhaps had your dad been more successful in his acting career, then he wouldn't have been in that accident.'

I couldn't believe she was bad-mouthing Dad! And how dare she blame his acting career on what had happened! I seriously had to resist the urge to use my powers to shake out all the flakes from the chilli-flakes shaker on to Auntie Cleo's head!

'My dad is a very good actor!' I said to her through gritted teeth and soya cheese. 'He might not have had any big parts in films or TV shows but we're still proud of him and proud of whatever job he does.'

'Oh, I wasn't trying to be scathing or anything, I was just—'

'Why did you have to come here?!' I blurted out angrily. 'I don't think my dad would even want you in our house.'

Auntie Cleo looked taken aback. 'I came to support you through this difficult time,' she said, her voice shifting uneasily. 'I'm sorry if I upset you.' She leaned across the table to touch my hand, but I snatched it away. She pulled her arm back awkwardly, then stood up. 'I'm just going to nip to the toilet.'

'I swear Auntie Cleo has just come here to cause trouble,' I said to my siblings.

'I think you're overreacting,' said Moaner.

'No, I'm not! And I dare you to spell overreacting.'

'O-v-e—'

'Look, I just don't want her staying with us, all right? She's horrid and she's trying to take over!'

'How?' asked Moaner.

'She … just is, OK?'

I said nothing more to Auntie Cleo for the remainder of the evening, but when I was pouring myself a glass of water before bed, Auntie Cleo apologised again.

'I think we might've got off on the wrong foot, Sonny,' she said. 'Seeing as I'm going to be staying here for a while, I would like us to get on. So again, I'm very sorry if I upset you in any way.'

I gave her a feeble nod to make out that I forgave her, when really, I didn't. And as I watched her take out the clothes that were in the washing machine to hang on the line outside, another chore I wanted to do tomorrow before school, it made me wish even more that Dad could wake up and come home, because I'm sure he'd be the first person to tell Auntie Cleo to get lost!

CHAPTER 33

'I need to get rid of my aunt,' I told Elliot when I went back to school the next day.

'You mean like BURY her in QUICKSAND or throw her into a PIT of DEADLY SNAKES?!'

'Of course not like that,' I said, rolling my eyes. 'I just want her to go back to her own home and stay out of mine!'

'What's she done?'

'She's not letting me do anything, that's what! Last night I wanted to make dinner, but she wanted to take us out for pizza. She did all my chores, *and* she finished my almond milk when, as far as I know, she doesn't have any food allergies!'

'I think your aunt sounds great! She takes you out for pizza, she does your chores, who wouldn't want that?'

said Elliot. 'I'd be over the moon if someone else wanted to do my chores for me.'

'She also said mean stuff about my dad, so trust me, she's not great. And anyway, I actually want to do my chores, so I don't need *her* doing them for me. Plus, I want to be the person looking out for Ramona and Oscar, which I know my dad would want. And that's the kind of stuff superheroes do, isn't it? Look out for people.'

I was hoping that we'd get to go to the hospital again, but when I got home from school, Auntie Cleo said she was going to take us all clothes shopping. It was Ramona who wanted to buy a new dress for Dad's eventual welcome home party.

We went to a shop on the high street, but it was so annoying having to wait for Ramona to decide what outfit she wanted, after she spent ages trying on loads of clothes before finally settling on a sparkly green dress. Oscar also picked out a shirt for himself. I wasn't interested in Auntie Cleo buying me new clothes so I left the shop empty-handed. Afterwards, we went to another restaurant called Delmere Burger, for burgers and chips.

'Delmere really hasn't changed. Take this restaurant, for example. It's been here for decades and the decor is pretty much how it's always been,' Auntie Cleo said to us.

'Then there's The Archer. The building looks as creepy as ever, especially with that hideous statue on the roof. It was derelict for a while before it became a health club, but before that, it used to be a factory that made buttons, and even back then we used to speculate if that was just a front and it was a whole other place entirely.'

'What did you think it was?' asked Ramona.

Auntie Cleo lowered her voice. 'We'd say it was really an evil laboratory where they extracted people's brains and pickled them in jars.' She giggled. 'That was one of several scary stories my friends and I would tell each other when we were kids.'

'I hate scary stories,' I muttered as I squeezed out a huge dollop of ketchup on to my chips, but I was semi-interested to hear that, like me, Auntie Cleo also thought The Archer was something more sinister.

'Would you ever move back to Delmere?' Ramona asked Auntie Cleo.

'Um, probably not, if I'm being honest,' she replied.

'Why? Is Delmere too boring for you?' I said sarcastically, even though I thought it was boring.

'No, I wouldn't call Delmere boring, especially as there's more than meets the eye with this town.'

'How d'you mean?' I asked.

'You probably wouldn't believe it if I told you.'

'Believe what?' I pressed, taking a bite out of my hamburger.

'Well, it is a very, *very* old town, which has had its fair share of urban myths.'

I put down my hamburger. 'Such as?'

Auntie Cleo lowered her voice again. 'Legend has it there are kids in this town who've had superpowers.'

'Superpowers!' gasped Ramona, though I pretended not to look as fascinated.

'Sonny says he has superpowers, but I don't believe him,' said Oscar.

'I was just joking, Osc,' I retorted, as Auntie Cleo threw me the same curious look that she'd given me when Mrs Armstrong said the same thing.

'So what exact powers do you have?' she asked me.

For a moment Auntie Cleo's face looked deadly serious, as though she didn't think I'd been joking, but then she started to laugh.

'Let me guess. You can stop time.' She smiled.

'Actually, I can move things with my mind,' I mumbled.

'Really?' said Auntie Cleo keenly.

'And you said you could fly,' Oscar chimed in.

I was the one now laughing, though it was more nervous laughter than anything. 'I meant that would be the kind of powers I'd want if I did have superpowers, but I don't. Nobody does,' I said.

'Well, I think both flying and being able to move things with one's mind would be excellent superpowers,' said Auntie Cleo, her eyes still fixed on me with intrigue.

Later on, I found myself wondering if the urban myth Auntie Cleo had mentioned was true, that there'd been kids in Delmere with superpowers like me. Maybe Auntie Cleo had known someone with powers, and that was why she constantly wanted to talk about it. But I certainly wasn't ready to tell her my secret, not when I still didn't like her.

CHAPTER 34

On Sunday, I was so looking forward to seeing Mum that throughout the morning I kept asking Auntie Cleo what time her plane would be landing. We were expecting her to be home by around seven in the evening, but at half past twelve Auntie Cleo got a call from Mum. I noticed a look of concern on Auntie Cleo's face before she hurriedly went upstairs with her phone. Some minutes later she came back down and said Mum wanted to do a FaceTime with me by myself. So I took the iPad to my room and sat on my bed. As Mum appeared on the screen, she looked nervous.

'Hi, Mum, will you be coming to the house first when you land or are you going to the hospital to see Dad?' I immediately asked. 'We all went to see him yesterday again. I talked and read a few chapters to him from my book about Jupiter, and Ramona read him this short story she'd written. It was about a princess called Ramonza who had to rescue her dad, the King, from a group of goblins who had taken over the kingdom by putting the King and almost everyone else to sleep …' I found myself waffling, but I just sensed that something wasn't right.

'Sonny, I know you're not going to like what I'm about to say, but I want you to know that I love you so, so much.' Mum took a deep breath as my heart began to pound. 'I'm really sorry, sweetheart, but I've decided that I'm not going to come home, not yet anyway,' she said through the screen.

'Why not?' I uttered, feeling totally deflated.

'It's hard to explain, but I just don't think I can handle seeing your dad in the state that he's in right now. That's why I think it's best I remain in Jordan and continue working.'

My head started to hurt with confusion.

'It sounds like you're abandoning us and abandoning Dad!'

'No, I'm not abandoning you, and I really do want to be home so I can support you and your siblings, and be there for your dad, but I'm just not good at dealing with tough situations.' She paused for a moment. 'It was the same for me when my dad died, and I was too upset to go to his funeral.'

Until now, I didn't quite know the full story of why my mum didn't go to my Grandpa Linton's funeral.

'Are you saying that Dad's going to die, and you don't want to be here when it happens?' I said, tears beginning to sting my eyes.

'No, sweetheart, that's not what I'm saying at all. I one hundred per cent believe your dad will wake up from his coma. The thing is, I want to be the best mum I can be to you, Ramona and Oscar, but I'm worried that if I come home, I'll struggle to do that. I'm scared I'll fall apart ...' Mum's voice trailed away, and she cleared her throat.

'But you said you were coming home today,' I replied miserably.

'I know I did and I'm really sorry.'

'We need you, Mum. Please just come home, please.'

'I can't, sweetheart,' she murmured, her eyes glassing with tears. 'I'm so sorry.'

She ended the FaceTime, the screen going blank, but it was like she'd thrown a grenade through it and let it explode around me. I sat in a daze.

It was as if my mum no longer cared about us.

There was a knock on my door.

'What?' I snapped.

'Sonny. Can I come in?' said Auntie Cleo.

'OK,' I murmured slowly.

Auntie Cleo came in and perched herself on my desk.

'I take it your mum's told you then, that she's not coming home yet.'

I glanced at Auntie Cleo blankly.

'She loves you so much,' she said gently. 'I know you're probably feeling devastated right now that your mum wants to stay in Jordan, but the thing you have to understand is, some people just handle upsetting situations differently and although this might not make any sense—'

'My mum doesn't care about us!' I cried.

'Oh, she does, Sonny, and if she could, she'd walk the length of this earth just to protect you, Ramona and Oscar – and Adam. It's just that she needs to be in a different environment right now, so she can come to terms with what's happening. But you don't have to worry, I'm going to take good care of you all.' She smiled softly. 'I know it's a hard time for everyone at the moment, and your dad is going to need all our love and support, Sonny. I want you to know, no matter how you're feeling about things, you can always come and talk to me. I like to think I'm a good listener, so if there's anything – and I mean *anything* – that you might want to tell me, then don't feel that you can't.'

I nodded sullenly.

'And is there anything you'd like to tell me? Perhaps something you've recently discovered.'

She looked at me searchingly and for a moment I wondered if Auntie Cleo had worked out I have superpowers.

'Like what?' I replied carefully.

'Um, like a … new star in the sky. Astronomers are always discovering these types of things, aren't they?'

I shrugged. 'I don't know of any new ones.'

'OK, well, as I said, if there is anything you want to talk about, I'm here.'

'Thanks,' I replied quietly.

'If you don't mind, I'd like to take the iPad as I know your mum's planning to call again so she can tell Ramona and Oscar her news. I expect they'll be pretty heart-broken too.'

I handed her the iPad.

'Listen, I know you're feeling upset, but I also know that you happen to love chilli con carne, as do Ramona and Oscar,' said Auntie Cleo.

I nodded slowly.

'Well, I hope you like my version, because I want to make it for dinner tonight and I'm hoping it'll help put a smile on everyone's faces,' said Auntie Cleo.

Her chilli con carne wasn't half bad, as it goes. To tell you the truth, it was even better than my mum's. But seeing both Ramona and Oscar in floods of tears after Mum had told them she wouldn't be coming home left me feeling really cross with her decision. And to me, it was the worst decision she could ever make.

CHAPTER 35

The next morning I was still angry about Mum not coming home, but I tried my best not to let Ramona and Oscar see. Auntie Cleo allowed me to make everyone breakfast when I asked if I could do it, and I decided to make pancakes. Even though my pancakes were yummy, they weren't enough to lift my mood and I left the house still fuming, so much so that I didn't bother to wait for Elliot at the bus stop like usual.

Let him find his own way there for a change, I thought.

As I arrived at school, I walked past the east entrance where Milo and his goons were patrolling and headed for the west entrance. But then I stopped and turned back round.

I was going to use the east entrance, and Milo was not going to stop me!

I was so full of ANGER and ADRENALIN that I didn't even think about the bombardment of chewing-gum missiles I was about to face.

As I approached the path, I could see Milo talking to some girls in his year. One of them was called Kayla. Apparently Milo had a crush on her; that's what Delilah told me anyway. Both Milo and Kayla were laughing at something he was showing her on his phone and seeing his smarmy face made it feel like the perfect moment to finally get my own back.

My brain buzzed like an alarm clock as I focused my mind on his phone. I made it slip out of his hand and crash heavily to the ground. Milo and his gang gasped, as did Kayla and her friend.

'OMIGOD! You've broken it!' said Kayla as she picked the phone up.

Oops! I didn't know it was hers.

'Why did you do that, Milo?' she shouted, her voice sounding like she was close to tears.

'I-I-I don't know ... I-i-t just fell. It was an accident,' he replied, trying to explain.

'You'll have to pay for her to get a new one now, because that phone cost a lot of money,' said Kayla's friend.

'I'm really sorry, Kayla,' said Milo.

'Oh, I don't want to hear it, you idiot!' she yelled, then stormed off with her friend.

'I'll give you the money for a new phone, I swear,' Milo called after her.

'Bro, that was not cool,' said Omar, shaking his head at him. He walked off with Charlie and Aiden, leaving Milo all by himself, his face looking both shocked and embarrassed.

Looks like I'd cost Milo a potential girlfriend too. Oh well, it served him right!

'I'm such a butterfingers!' Milo scolded himself, his head in his hands. He didn't notice me walking past.

Elliot had no sympathy for Milo when I told him what I'd done, but he did have lots of sympathy for me when I told him how my mum had decided not to come home. Which meant he wasn't too annoyed that I hadn't waited for him at the bus stop.

'I'd be sad too if my mum had some horrible aunt looking after me,' he said as we sat in our form class.

'Actually, my aunt's kinda cool, and right now, I think she's much nicer than my mum.'

I was starting to change my mind about Auntie Cleo. She wasn't as horrid as I thought. I guess I just hadn't given her a chance.

CHAPTER 36

When the bell went for the end of school, I was still feeling angry and upset, and this made me not want to go home straight away, so as I dawdled along the street, I found myself outside The Archer. I stared at the building with curiosity, watching as someone was buzzed in. I tried to catch a glimpse inside as the door was opened, although I couldn't see anything. I don't know why, but I just wanted to investigate the place – not that I've done any type of investigating before, unless you count me trying to solve my BIG DREAM MYSTERY when I was still wondering if my powers were real.

I tried my best to look inconspicuous as I casually kicked a drink can that was on the pavement. I kicked it all the way to the back of the building, which I'd not seen before. There were a few cars parked, as well as the bins. There was a fire escape staircase going up four storeys, and at the top of the stairs I could see the door was open.

Should I take a peek inside? I wondered. But then I thought, *What if The Archer really is the headquarters of some scary secret society and I get trapped inside? What if they really do extract people's brains?*

However, I was feeling bold, even bolder than this morning when I got my own back on Milo. So I wasted no time in climbing the stairs, and when I reached the door, I took a cautious step inside. Slowly I walked down the corridor towards a glass door at the end. There were two men moving large boxes in what looked like a dance studio; or was it?

I tried to see if there was anything about the men that gave the game away that they were suspicious or abnormal. They might be shapeshifting aliens with little antennas sticking out of their heads. Though they looked like regular people. Still, they could've just been very deceptive shapeshifting aliens, and who's to say those boxes didn't contain brain-extraction devices?

One of the men suddenly spotted me. I gulped as he started charging towards the door and I quickly ran off as fast as I could.

'Oi, you! What do you think you're doing?' the man shouted after me.

As I headed back out, I bounded frantically down the stairs, and when I got to the bottom, the man was leaning against the railing, looking down at me.

'This place is for members only!' he yelled.

I gulped again before running off once more, and I don't know why, but I just kept running and running until I eventually came to a road that was curved, so you couldn't see the houses at the end of it. When I looked at the street sign, I realised I was on the road where Dad had his accident – Chalingsford Lane. And a few metres up the street was a yellow sign that said 'ACCIDENT' and 'CAN YOU HELP?' And I just knew it was Dad's accident it was referring to.

I walked towards it. Sure enough, the sign had the date and the time of Dad's accident and a telephone number for people to call. My anger grew until the only thing I could feel was SHEER RAGE!

I looked around, checking that the coast was clear, and after watching a man and his dog go into one of the houses, I launched upwards, soaring as high as the clouds, so no one could see me or at least make out that a human boy was flying.

I tore through the sky with speed, flying over numerous houses, then fields, then the village of Shillbrook, flying over cottages with thatched roofs, including the cottage Dad grew up in.

I didn't stop flying until I reached the Shillbrook mountains. It's a place where Dad and I have gone hiking a few times, just the two of us. And as my feet touched the ground, I followed the rocky path that led to a stream, picking up stones on my way. When I got to the stream, I took off my rucksack and sat on the marsh. I took out my phone and immediately called Mum's mobile. It went straight to voicemail, and as the bleep sounded, I hesitated, struggling to get the words that were in my head out of my mouth. So I hung up without saying anything and switched off my phone altogether. I then started to throw the stones into the water one by one.

'How can you just abandon us, Mum?' I cried, finally able to get the words out.

I threw another stone.

'It's not fair on Dad, or me, or Ramona and Oscar.'

When I threw my next stone, I used my powers to make it skim the water, the stone bouncing several metres high, over and over, before I allowed it to sink.

'Dad might die, and you won't be there. What will you do then, huh? What am I going to do!'

Tears gathered in my eyes.

This was the voicemail I would've left had I not hung up. Words which probably would've left Mum feeling worse than she was already feeling. But I didn't

171

want to make my mum feel even more upset. I just wanted her to come home, that's all.

I swivelled my head round and stared at the mountains. I got up and flew right to the very top. And as I stood on one of the mountains, taking in the epic landscape, I suddenly SCREAMED and SCREAMED, and the landscape screamed back. Tears poured down my face, and with every new scream I released, slowly my anger began to dissolve. When I eventually stopped and thought of Mum again, I didn't feel so cross with her any more and wished I could've told her how much I loved her.

I let out a heavy sigh, and the landscape copied.

All at once a thought popped into my head as I looked towards the other mountain.

Could I move these mountains? I wondered.

It would surely be the ultimate test of my powers.

I nodded to myself, then rose high above the mountains.

You can do this, Sonny.

As I took a deep breath, I focused my mind on the two mountains, a buzzing sound filling my head again.

Move.

Suddenly the earth below me began to rumble.

Move.

The earth shook harder, but none of this was feeling easy. I intensified my focus, my arms outstretched.

Move.

Rocks started to fall and crumble.

Move.

My whole body tensed as I used all my brain power.

One. Last. Try.

I clenched my jaw as the buzzing sound in my head grew louder. Then, suddenly and slowly, the mountains began to draw apart.

Yes!

I'd moved the Shillbrook mountains!

I whooped with joy, knowing I'd achieved something beyond my wildest imagination. My powers were truly the greatest, and if I could move these mountains, perhaps I could even move Mount Kilimanjaro or the tallest mountain in the world, Mount Everest! Hey, maybe I could even move the moon and all the planets in the solar system! How awesome would that be? I imagine it would cause a lot of chaos for mankind, though – and alien-kind.

Afterwards I began the process of putting the mountains back in their original position, and I was feeling properly exhausted and hungry. So I got ready to teleport home, but then, out of nowhere, a sharp ringing sound ripped through my ears as my body began to wobble. I recognised this feeling and quickly gripped hold of a rock beside me, clinging on as tightly as I could to stop myself from going to that one place I didn't want to be. But it was no use, because within a flash I'd returned to The Stuck Place.

CHAPTER 37

I felt as though I'd fallen through a crack in the earth, and once again I couldn't move my arms and legs. I could hear the not-so-distant voice of Mrs Moretti, who was asking Mr Donohue if he'd be interested in taking her old microwave for scrap as she was planning to get a new one.

'HELP!' I hollered, even though I knew they wouldn't be able to hear me.

The Stuck Place felt scarier than the first time I landed here, and the cold, expansive darkness had me completely trapped.

'I have a feeling he's not telling me everything,' said a voice that I immediately recognised as Auntie Cleo's.

Her voice sounded much clearer than Mr Donohue's,

which made me think I must've been right outside my house.

'If it does turn out to be true, then we stand a great chance of pulling this off,' Auntie Cleo went on.

Who was she talking to?

I couldn't hear anyone else, so perhaps she was on the phone.

'I do feel our luck is about to come in, and I can't wait to celebrate.'

Celebrate what?

'Sonny isn't home yet. I thought he'd be back already, and it looks like he's switched off his phone.'

Was Auntie Cleo talking to Mum?

Perhaps they were talking about Dad. Maybe he'd woken up, so she couldn't wait to celebrate his return at his welcome home party. Yippee! And maybe this meant Mum was coming home too, meaning I had to get out of The Stuck Place right away!

But I knew I had to wait, just like the last time I was here. At least my excitement about Dad waking up from his coma helped me to feel less afraid.

'Bye, speak soon,' said Auntie Cleo. Then I think she must have gone back inside the house, because I couldn't hear her any more.

After what felt like an hour of just floating, once again it was as if blinds were being opened just a tiny bit all around me, as light filtered in. Then I began wobbling vigorously, and as more light came in, I could see myself. It was like I'd become part of an echo, my body creating hundreds of other Sonnys. A moment later, I began to fall, and it felt like I was tumbling down from tens of metres before I landed flat on my lawn. I immediately dashed to the door, frantically opening it with my keys. I ran straight to the living room.

'Has Dad woken up?' I asked Auntie Cleo straight away.

'Sonny! I've been trying to contact you,' she said, getting up from the sofa.

'Because my dad's awake, right?' I said fervently.

'Um, no, there's no change I'm afraid. It was just getting late, and I wanted to know where you were,' said Auntie Cleo.

My stomach dropped with disappointment as tears filled my eyes again.

'But I want him to be better so he can come home, and my mum as well,' I whimpered. 'I miss them so much, Auntie Cleo.'

'I know you do, Sonny,' she said, putting her arm around me as I sobbed uncontrollably.

CHAPTER 38

I couldn't stop wondering who Auntie Cleo had been talking to on the phone.

What was it that she was hoping to pull off?

I wanted to ask her, but I needed to think of a way I could without letting her know about my ability to teleport.

'Have you spoken to my mum today?' I casually asked as I helped her wash the dishes later that evening.

'No I haven't, but I did send her a text earlier,' she replied.

'Did Mrs Armstrong pop over or have you spoken to her today?'

'Was she planning to pop over?'

I shrugged. 'I just wondered.'

'Well, she didn't, and I haven't spoken to her either.'

'So nobody's called then?'

Auntie Cleo looked at me inquisitively. 'My boss at work called, so it's just been her and your dad's doctor at the hospital who I've spoken to today.'

So Auntie Cleo must have been talking about a work thing, then.

'Why are you so interested to know who's called?' she asked.

'Because … I was hoping the hospital would call you to say Dad was awake,' I decided to say.

'Oh, Sonny, I wish the doctor had told me that. I do know how much you want to get that news and I'm hoping it'll be very soon,' said Auntie Cleo softly.

Just then, her phone buzzed. She dried her hands and sat at the kitchen table reading the text message she'd been sent.

'Is that a message from Mum?' I asked.

'No, it's just a text from a friend.'

Then suddenly Auntie Cleo gasped.

'What is it?' I said, turning round.

'I've just got a news alert. There was an EARTHQUAKE today at the Shillbrook mountains!'

'An earthquake? Wow,' I said, trying to keep my voice steady, even though I knew it was me who'd caused it, and straight away I hoped nobody had been hurt.

'Was anyone hurt?' I asked slowly.

'No, it doesn't look like it.'

I let out a small sigh of relief.

'This article I'm reading doesn't say how big the earthquake was, but apparently it was felt in the village,' said Auntie Cleo. 'I know this isn't the only strange thing to have happened in these parts recently,' she continued. 'I know about the tornado in Ocean View, which makes it all feel so eerily familiar.'

'How do you mean?'

'Oh, there's always some year or another when the weather is totally weird.' Auntie Cleo smiled quickly. 'Look, how's about I finish the washing-up while you go and watch some telly?'

'I don't mind finishing it.'

'You don't have to feel like you need to be helping out all the time, you know,' she said. 'You should be having fun, Sonny – playing video games, watching TV, and more importantly doing your homework. You only get to be a kid once in this life so you should be making the most of it.'

'OK.' I nodded. 'But I think I'll save my homework until later. I'll watch some telly first.'

'Good,' said Auntie Cleo, with another smile.

'I'll just send my mum a text first.'

And that text said: *Hope you're doing OK. Don't worry about me not getting on with Auntie C. I think she's cool. Love you x*

CHAPTER 39

'I wish I could work out a way of avoiding The Stuck Place,' I said to Elliot as we hung out in Fern Park the following day after school. 'I've been thinking that maybe why I randomly get trapped there is because I'm teleporting so fast that time simply can't keep up with me.'

'Hmm, possibly. Though, one thing you could do if you get stuck there again is to have the flashlight on your phone switched on. At least that way you'll be able to see in the dark,' said Elliot.

'Yeah, but that won't exactly stop me from going to The Stuck Place,' I said.

Elliot looked at me studiously for a second. 'Hey, you know how you said that you feel like you're floating in The Stuck Place?'

'Uh-huh.'

'Well, what other stuff have you noticed?'

'Time always feels much slower there and whenever I manage to get out, I always feel like I'm falling.'

'Hmm. I reckon that if The Stuck Place is, say, somewhere that's between time and space, and you're the only person who can see it, then perhaps it's a place that sits above our reality.'

'Really? And where did you get an idea like that from?'

'There was a film I watched recently with my dad. It was about a man who could teleport just like you, and he could teleport to these different dimensions which were literally above his head that only he could see.'

'And how does this tie into me trying to avoid The Stuck Place?'

'I'm about to get to that part,' said Elliot. 'What I think you should do is try sitting on the ground when you teleport, so you don't float up to The Stuck Place.'

'But I don't ever feel like I'm floating up to it. I just appear there,' I said.

'Well, it's just a theory,' Elliot replied, and blew out his cheeks.

However, I did take a few moments to consider his idea. 'I suppose I could try sitting and see if that changes anything,' I said eventually.

But to be honest, I wasn't that convinced it would work.

Elliot and I walked to an empty part of the park so I could put his theory to the test. I sat on the grass and placed the palms of my hands down as well.

'I'm going to teleport myself to that tree over there,' I said to Elliot, pointing to a large oak tree nearby.

And as I got ready to teleport, with the tree pictured in my head, my arms and legs began to tingle. A split second later I was sitting beside it.

'It worked! I didn't go to The Stuck Place!' I called out to Elliot. 'I'll give it another go and teleport to that tree,' I added, pointing towards another.

As I pictured the second tree in my mind, my body began to wobble, while a familiar ringing sound returned to my ears. As quick as a flash, I was back in The Stuck Place.

I didn't bother trying to move because I knew there'd be no use. I just had to wait. I was also floating again, so sitting down hadn't made a single difference. I could hear Elliot's voice.

'Are you still there, Sonny?' he kept saying.

Very soon, although it still felt like hours in The Stuck Place, light began to stream in and I was able to see out through tiny gaps. I could just about make out Elliot, who appeared to be swinging his arms above his head.

As more light filtered in, my body began to wobble, faster and faster, and not a moment too soon I was falling once again, landing on the grass.

'There you are!' said Elliot, sprinting over to me. 'So I take it you found yourself in The Stuck Place again?'

I nodded. 'Your theory didn't work. As usual, the whole place was pitch black, then some light started coming in, and I could see you. Then after that, I was falling out of it again,' I explained. 'By the way, why were you swinging your arms about?'

'I was trying to see if I could reach into The Stuck Place, make the invisible visible and pull you out, if that makes sense.'

'Maybe The Stuck Place isn't above us, because it's not as if I'm looking down when I'm seeing the outside world.'

'I really think you should test my original theory and turn on your phone's flashlight, because from what you're saying, it sounds like you're only able to escape when the light starts coming in.'

'Yeah, and that's normally when my body starts to wobble,' I said, and wobbled my body to demonstrate.

Elliot giggled, then went back to looking deep in thought.

'It sounds like The Stuck Place doesn't like light,' he said, 'just like, um … ice doesn't like salt because salt helps to melt it!'

'I think I get what you're saying,' I responded. 'All right, I'll give that a try this time.'

I took my phone out of my trouser pocket and put on the flashlight. I stared at the first oak tree to where I'd teleported and pictured it in my head again. My body started to tingle and I teleported straight to the tree. Next, I focused on another tree and quickly teleported to it, no problem. I continued this twice more.

'I think you might be on to something,' I said to Elliot.

When I went to teleport again, my body started to wobble, but only a little bit, and for a second everything was dark, then the next second it was super bright, then I was standing beside the tree.

Had I briefly landed in The Stuck Place?

I told Elliot what had happened.

'Not to sound all Star Wars-y, but it sounds like the light was able to destroy the dark, which is why you were able to quickly get out of The Stuck Place,' he said.

'Yeah, that's not a bad way of putting it,' I replied.

I continued to test his hypothesis, teleporting back and forth between the trees, several times over. Only once, for a fleeting moment, did I find myself surrounded by the dark again, followed by a brief and brilliant brightness before I appeared next to the tree. So it was like the light had catapulted me out of the dark.

'It looks like I will need to have the flashlight on when I teleport,' I said to Elliot.

But for me, it was a BIG relief, and hopefully it meant I'd never get trapped in The Stuck Place again.

CHAPTER 40

During the week we made some more trips to the hospital to see Dad, mostly after school. I'd brought along more of my space books to read to him, like my book on constellations. I also told him how I was looking forward to us doing some stargazing again, as well as playing our highly competitive games of *Scrabble*. And I reminisced about other father-son bonding that we've done, like the time we decorated my bedroom with wallpaper that's of a spectacular nebula.

On Sunday, Ramona and I told Dad how we'd helped Auntie Cleo out with some of the cooking. The day before we'd helped her make Jamaican patties and toto, which is a coconut cake that tastes really delicious. Oscar, however, was being a right pain, for some reason.

He kept trying to shove Ramona out of the easy chair they were sharing. Then, when we got back home and had a FaceTime with Mum, he kept hogging the iPad, meaning Ramona and I didn't get as much time to chat with her.

As it was a warm and sunny day, Auntie Cleo decided we'd have a barbecue, and we ate barbecue chicken and burgers in the garden. I thought Oscar might've calmed down, but he continued to be really annoying, and later on I caught him rifling around my bedroom, making a huge mess.

'What are you doing, Oscar?' I snapped.

'I'm trying to find Zed, my Power Piglet. He's my favourite.'

'I'm getting fed up with you leaving your Power Piglets in my room. You'd better clean up this mess.'

Oscar didn't respond as he rummaged through my chest of drawers, pulling out all my socks and undies and throwing them on to the floor.

'Will you just stop, Oscar?! You're seriously getting on my nerves now. I doubt that horrible piglet is even in there.'

'My Power Piglets are not horrible!' Oscar blared, then went over to my wardrobe. He swung the door open so forcefully that it slammed into my telescope, sending it crashing into the wall.

'OSCAR!'

I quickly checked my telescope and could see there was a tiny crack in the lens. I was furious!

'You've damaged it, Oscar!' I shouted. 'Just get out of my room!'

Oscar ran out while I sat angrily on my bed with my arms folded.

How would he like it if I broke his things?

'I've found him!' said Oscar, coming back into my room holding his dumb toy. 'Zed was in my wardrobe.'

'So now you can clean up my room.'

'Why should I? It's not my room.'

'But you're the one who made this mess. So clean it up now!'

'No, *you* do it!' he retorted, and ran back out again.

'Those grotty Power Piglets belong in the bin!' I yelled after him.

Right now, I hated those Power Piglets with all my heart and I would've loved nothing better than to see them gone. And as these feelings of anger flowed through me, I focused my mind on a thought of Oscar's Power Piglets floating away and millions more piglets, all over the world, my brain buzzing like a swarm of mosquitoes.

'ZED!' I heard Oscar suddenly screech from downstairs.

I went out to the landing as three of his other Power

Piglets barged past me, each of them gliding out of the open window in the bathroom.

I secretly smiled, but as I came down the stairs there was a look of amazement on Oscar's face as he opened the front door, Auntie Cleo and Ramona following behind.

And despite knowing what I'd done, I couldn't help being stunned at the sight of what greeted us outside. In the sky, as far as the eye could see, were Power Piglets. In a strange sort of way, it was a beautiful sight. Well, as beautiful as fluffy piglets in capes get.

'What is this?!' said Auntie Cleo, not quite believing her eyes. Then she looked at me. 'One minute Oscar was holding his Power Piglet, then the next it was dashing out of the living-room window, I guess to join all those other ones.'

'Looks like pigs really can fly,' I heard Mr Donohue say, amongst the neighbours who had gathered in the middle of the street, all of them looking up at this great spectacle. Though Mrs Moretti's four-year-old daughter Sofia was crying, which made me feel rotten.

'My Gavin is inside bawling his eyes out!' I heard Miss Lister say to Mrs Okaru and Mrs Silva from number 28. 'I was taking in a parcel when suddenly I felt something going over my shoulder, and lo and behold, it was Gavin's Power Piglet!'

'My old Power Piglet is up there too,' I heard Blessing say to Ramona.

Blessing had Noodle with her, who was barking up at the sky. I guess, like everyone else, Noodle was trying to work out what the CRUSTY BREADCRUMBS was going on.

'Do you think they'll come back down?' Blessing asked her dad, who was standing next to her.

'Well, if they do, I don't think you or any kid should be playing with them. It's clear there's a serious manufacturing fault,' said Mr Okaru, while at the same time trying to shush Noodle.

'Do you think they've got helium in them?' said Mrs Okaru.

'Well, whatever they've got inside them, Eunice, all I know is that I want my money back!' replied Mrs Silva.

'My Josh's piglet went straight through the roof! And just look at the state of it!' Mr Irvine from number 25 said to everyone as he pointed up at his house.

My stomach began to churn with guilt, especially as Mr Irvine's house wasn't the only one to have a hole in the roof.

'They'd have to have a lot more than helium in them if they were able to do that kind of damage,' said Miss Lister to Mrs Okaru and Mrs Silva. 'Titanium maybe?'

'Josh was holding the toy at the time. What if he'd burst through the roof with it?' said Mr Irvine, shaking his head. 'Honestly, it doesn't bear thinking about! One thing I do know is that the bosses at that corporation will be sweating like pigs once I've sued the tails off them, you mark my word!'

'Yes, I expect they'll be in a whole lot of pig poo after this debacle,' said Mrs Moretti, chucking in her own pig idiom.

'It's so weird how all the Power Piglets floated off at the same time,' Ramona said.

I swallowed. 'Yeah, I guess it is,' I murmured.

'Could it be …' I heard Auntie Cleo say to herself as she stared at the piglets. Her eyes met mine, and for a moment she held my gaze, another curious look on her face, before she looked back up at the sky.

'Social media is going *crazy* right now! It looks like there are Power Piglets in the sky all over the world!' said Ryan, Mr Irvine's eldest son.

Despite all the trouble I was causing, it was remark-able to know that my powers could TRANSCEND THE WORLD! But I knew I had to stop this. I'd let my anger go too far. So in my mind, I imagined all the Power Piglets in the world floating down to the ground as I focused on the ones above me. My mind started to buzz again as all the piglets I could see across the neighbourhood began to fall. A few people clapped, while Mrs Moretti shrieked as she scooped Sofia away from the plummeting piglets.

'But they're coming back, Mummy,' said Sofia, with a big smile on her face.

As soon as they reached the ground, Oscar quickly grabbed his piglets, though there was some confusion amongst a few of the kids as to which Power Piglet belonged to whom.

One of the piglets had to be prised from Noodle's jaw, who looked very excited and determined to hold on to it. She probably thought all of her birthdays had come at once, getting to have her pick of these soft toys.

'Let's just get back inside,' said Auntie Cleo, and as she ushered us indoors, I was feeling really awful about what I'd done.

So I made a pact with myself, there and then, that I'd never use my powers when I was feeling angry or use them as a way of getting back at people, even the likes of Milo Allerton. Plus, there'd be no more of me moving cars and *definitely* no more moving mountains. But it was nice seeing Oscar happy to have his Power Piglets back, and I made sure I apologised to him for my earlier antics.

'I'm sorry I shouted at you, Osc,' I told him.

'It's OK,' he replied, not even sounding that interested as he enjoyed a group hug with his piglets.

But I felt like I needed to make it up to him. 'Would you like me to get you some ice cream from the freezer? I can put some toffee sauce on it if you like.'

'Yes, please,' said Oscar, smiling.

I went to the kitchen. Auntie Cleo was sitting at the table, looking deep in thought.

'Is everything all right?' I asked.

She looked at me as she tapped her fingers together.

'I think it's happening again,' she muttered.

CHAPTER 41

'What's happening again?' I said, confused, as I joined Auntie Cleo at the table.

'Oh, ignore me. I'm being silly,' she quickly replied.

'But I can see you're concerned about something. Is it something to do with the Power Piglets?'

Auntie Cleo let out a sigh.

'I suppose there's no harm in telling you, considering I have kind of told you already,' she said. 'I've sort of seen something like this before.'

'Flying Power Piglets?'

She chuckled briefly, then said, 'No, other strange occurrences which all started to happen around the same time. 1988, to be exact. Remember the urban myth I told you about of there being kids in this town with superpowers?'

I nodded.

'Well, I don't believe it is a myth. I think it's all true.'

My eyes widened. 'Really? Have you met kids with superpowers?'

Auntie Cleo looked at me attentively. 'I was just a little older than you when I was out shopping one day with your Granny Daphne,' she began. 'We saw this little girl get hit by a car, which was such an awful sight, one that I've never been able to get out of my head. But the weird thing was, the girl got up from the crash and she didn't seem to have a single scratch on her. She looked a little shocked, but she seemed to be perfectly fine.'

'So the car didn't hit her then?'

'Oh, it hit her all right. I didn't know the girl, but apparently when she was taken to hospital and had X-rays done, she didn't have one broken bone, or even a sprain! The doctors said it was a miracle, but I knew there was more to it.'

'Like what?'

'Like the girl having a superpower of super-strength.'

I blinked more rapidly this time.

So there have been others with superpowers!

'You probably think I'm making all of this up.'

'No, I don't. It's very interesting,' I said. 'So do you know how the girl might've got her superpower?'

'Well, I was convinced that it had something to do with this town, especially after I heard about a cat that was found frozen in ice. And bizarrely, it happened on a day that was boiling hot after a kid was seen playing with the cat. Then there was a month when we had these constant blackouts across the town, and I remember my dad saying how the power network operator didn't seem to have a clue what was causing it. He also told me how one night when he was walking home, he saw a boy pointing at the street lamps, which were flashing on and off. He said it was as if the boy was controlling them.'

'So the boy had ... ELECTRICAL POWERS?!'

'That's what it sounded like. I also wouldn't be surprised if that same kid was responsible for the black-outs,' said Auntie Cleo. 'And then there was ...' She stopped herself from saying any more.

'What?'

Auntie Cleo lowered her eyes for a moment. 'This ... boy I knew.' She looked back at me. 'He was in my form at school. His name was George. He was a bit of a loner, but I'd speak to him now and again. Then one day George decided to reveal to me that he had a superpower. Of course, I didn't believe him until he showed me. One Sunday afternoon, we snuck into a closed timber yard and there were these planks of wood all piled high. There must have been at least three dozen, and George lifted them all.'

'He did?!' I said, my jaw falling open.

'George was someone else who was super strong. But him lifting those planks was nothing compared to the lorry I watched him pick up,' she said. 'So yeah, I believe there have been kids in this town, or at least in this county, who've had superpowers and I know I'm not the only one. There's even a name for this phenomenon. They call it the Delmere Magic.'

I was stunned by what Auntie Cleo was telling me.

Just how many other kids could there be with super-powers? I wondered.

'Where's my ice cream?' Oscar suddenly squawked.

I'd completely forgotten all about that.

'I'm just getting it now, Oscar,' I called, getting up from the table.

I went and took the tub of ice cream out of the freezer, and as I scooped some into a bowl, I started to think about my own powers. There surely had to be more to the story as to how I came to acquire them. So maybe there was a connection to the kids that Auntie Cleo was talking about.

After I'd finished squirting toffee sauce over Oscar's ice cream, I took it to the living room.

'Here you go,' I said, handing him the bowl.

'Thanks,' he replied, then went back to chatting with his Power Piglets.

I wondered whether to just come out with it and tell Auntie Cleo about my powers, because maybe she could help me work out where I'd got them from.

'You look like you've got something on your mind,' she said as I returned to the kitchen. 'But I completely understand if you're wondering whether I've lost the plot. I'm sure it sounds totally outlandish.'

'No, I believe you, Auntie Cleo.'

I sat back down at the table.

'I know someone with superpowers,' I murmured.

'Really? Who?' said Auntie Cleo, leaning forward.

I got up again and went over to the sink. I poured a glass of water, then brought it back to the table.

'Who do you know with superpowers?' she asked.

I stared at the glass of water, my mind buzzing silently. Straight away the water shot up and stayed suspended in the air.

'Oh my God!' Auntie Cleo gasped. 'How is that—'

'I did it,' I answered. 'I have superpowers, Auntie Cleo.'

CHAPTER 42

For a few minutes, Auntie Cleo just stared at the puddle of water that remained static in the air.

'So you're doing this?' she said eventually, looking stunned.

I nodded.

'I knew it!'

'You knew I had superpowers?'

'Um, no, what I meant is, it just reminds me of when I was younger and witnessed George and his super-power,' said Auntie Cleo. 'Though this definitely isn't a magic trick, is it?' she asked.

'No. I moved the water with my mind.'

'So, it is water?' said Auntie Cleo, sounding unsure.

'Yes.'

Very slowly she reached up and moved her hand across the water.

'It's wet,' she announced as though she'd only just discovered this very fact about water. 'Wow, you really do have a superpower!'

With my mind I made the water come back down into the glass.

'So do you want to tell me how this all works?' said Auntie Cleo.

'Well, first I have to picture the thing I want to move in my head, keeping myself calm, then focusing as hard as I can. Then whatever the thing is will begin to move,' I explained. 'I'm even able to move things that are far away.'

'Seriously?'

I nodded. 'It was me who made all the Power Piglets float up into the sky and I can move mountains, Auntie Cleo. No joke,' I said. Then, biting my lip guiltily, I added, 'It was me who caused the earthquake. I moved the Shillbrook mountains. I used my mind to pull them apart.'

'That was all you!' said Auntie Cleo, blinking rapidly.

'Do you reckon my power has got something to do with the Delmere Magic?' I asked her.

'Yes, I think it might, Sonny,' she replied. 'So is it just you with a superpower? Do Ramona and Oscar have abilities?'

I shook my head. 'No, just me. But telekinesis isn't my only power.'

'What else can you do?' said Auntie Cleo, looking surprisingly excited.

'I can fly and teleport,' I said, then demonstrated my flying abilities as I glided around the room, making Auntie Cleo gasp again.

'Oh my,' she muttered. She gave me a huge smile. 'This is outstanding, Sonny! I bet you must love having powers?'

'I do, but it's not always fun.'

'Why is that?' Auntie Cleo asked as I returned to the table.

'Well, my teleporting hasn't always worked properly. Sometimes when I've teleported, I've ended up in this strange place where I can't see anything or even move – well, not at first. It's like I'm stuck in another dimension, but I think I've now worked out a way to get myself out of there.'

'Oh good, because it certainly doesn't sound like a place one would want to find oneself in, and we can't have you getting stuck there when …' Auntie Cleo's voice fizzled out.

'What?'

'When we need you here with us, Sonny,' said Auntie Cleo. 'So tell me a bit more about this teleporting. Can you just teleport anywhere?'

I nodded.

'I take it your mum and dad don't know about your powers.'

'I was planning to tell my dad the day he had his accident, but now I want to wait until he wakes up so I can tell him and my mum together.'

'Does anyone else know?'

'I did tell Oscar and Ramona, and Mrs Armstrong, but they didn't believe me. So the only person who does properly know and has seen my powers for themselves is Elliot. But he's promised not to tell anyone.'

'OK,' said Auntie Cleo, nodding her head. She put her hands together, and I could see she was thinking carefully. 'Yes, I think it's best no one else knows about your powers just yet. There's too much risk.'

'Why do you say that?'

'It's to do with George,' said Auntie Cleo. 'Something he told me all those years ago.'

'What?'

'He told me that a company were after him.'

'What kind of company?'

'I really don't know, nor did George.'

'Was the company in Delmere?'

'George thought they were, but he didn't know where exactly.'

'What was the name of the company?'

'George seemed to think that they didn't have a name. You see, Sonny, they were the kind of organisation that operated in the shadows, who had somehow discovered that George had a superpower. They wanted to take it away from him,' said Auntie Cleo. 'George was so terrified that he'd get experimented on, that he and his mum fled town. Nobody knew where they went, and it was only by chance that I managed to see him again many years later.'

'Where did you see him?'

'When I went on holiday to Tenerife. He just so happened to be walking along the beach.'

'And did he say anything to you?'

'We chatted, yes, except I wasn't able to get much information out of him. He didn't want to tell me where he and his mum had vanished to, and I wasn't sure if he was living in Tenerife or was on holiday there himself. All he was willing to tell me was that his superpower had gone.'

'Gone?! So did the company catch up with him?'

'No.' Auntie Cleo shook her head. 'It seems his power had simply faded away. He said it happened when he turned eighteen. He told me he couldn't even lift a sofa without needing help.'

'And did he know why he lost his power?'

Auntie Cleo shook her head again. 'But I do think

that whatever led to him having a superpower is something that only kids can get. I guess they just grow out of it as they get older.'

'Does my mum know about the Delmere Magic?' I asked.

'No. She was the same age as Oscar back then. Thankfully, she didn't get to witness the little girl's accident as she was at home with your grandad, and I decided not to tell her about George because I thought the fewer people who knew about his superpower, the better.'

'I'd love to know how I got my powers. Maybe it does have something to do with this town. Maybe there are powerful electromagnetic waves or something that are giving kids powers.'

Auntie Cleo shrugged. 'There could be, but who knows?' She looked at me more seriously. 'I am however concerned, Sonny, that the company that was after George might still exist. I don't want to alarm you, but I'd hate to think what could happen if they were to find out you had powers. So you're going to need to stay on your guard, OK?'

My heart started to thud. I wouldn't want anyone taking my powers away. Then I thought about other kids who might have superpowers. They too could be at risk of having their powers stolen. All of us could be in danger!

CHAPTER 43

The flying Power Piglets were all over the news on TV, and when I popped into the newsagent's the next day before school, the Power Piglets were on the front page of every newspaper.

'WORLD BESIEGED BY FLYING PIGLETS,' screamed one newspaper headline. 'NOT AS HAPPY AS A PIG,' read another, over a photo of the chief executive of Power Piglets Inc. looking completely dumbfounded.

There were pictures from all over the world of the Power Piglets in the sky, and a few had famous landmarks in the background, such as the Sydney Opera House in Australia, the Empire State Building in New York, the Houses of Parliament in London, and the

Leaning Tower of Pisa in Italy. It was breathtaking to think I was responsible for all of it.

Power Piglets Inc. had recalled every Power Piglet in the world, and it was expected billions of pounds would be wiped off the corporation's share value, which one newspaper article I read said would 'likely affect the toy industry as a whole'. And with Power Piglets Inc. promising to refund all customers, and pay for any damage caused to people's homes, which of course was going to be massively expensive, the corporation was 'now facing an uncertain future' – all because of me! As I walked to the bus stop to wait for Elliot, I couldn't help feeling down about the mayhem I'd caused. All I'd wanted to do was teach Oscar a lesson, not cause an ECONOMIC MELTDOWN! On top of this, I now had to worry that there might be a sinister organisation out there wanting to steal my powers and those of other superpowered kids who most likely had no idea such a company might be after them. I decided that I'd try and find these kids so I could warn them. It'd also be a way I could do a good deed for a change, just as any superhero should, which I still wanted to be.

As soon as he got off the bus, the Power Piglets were the only thing Elliot wanted to talk about.

'I've been wondering what they might've put in the Power Piglets to make them fly. My mum and dad think someone took Phoebe's two piglets when they all came back down but I suppose that doesn't matter, now that they're being recalled,' said Elliot, completely unaware it was me who'd made the piglets fly. So I decided to come clean and tell him.

'It was you who caused a GLOBAL CATASTROPHE!' said Elliot, with a massive grin.

'Keep your voice down,' I hissed as we made our way into school. 'I was cross with Oscar, and even though I did imagine all the Power Piglets in the world floating away, I didn't think it would cause all this trouble.'

'Well, personally I'm pleased that you helped rid the world of those pesky piglets. I was so fed up with tripping over Phoebe's piglets all the time. But now it looks like the manufacturer won't be making any more. Hooray!' said Elliot, throwing his arms up. 'I also think it's awesome how you were able to use your mind to control every Power Piglet in the entire world,' he whispered.

I waited until lunchtime to tell Elliot what Auntie Cleo had told me about the Delmere Magic and the weird goings-on of 1988, as well as George and The Company. Plus, I told him that, like George, there could be a chance my powers wouldn't last beyond the age of eighteen.

'George had to leave Delmere and, by the sounds of it, go into hiding so that The Company wouldn't find him,' I told Elliot as we ambled around our school playing field. 'I'd hate it if I had to go into hiding.'

'Yeah, that would be a bummer if you had to do that,' he agreed. 'So your aunt's certain that kids lose their powers once they turn eighteen?'

'That's what this George person told her.'

The thought that my superpowers could just disappear made me feel quite sad. They might've been a bit hit-and-miss sometimes, but I still loved them. They'd become part of my identity, so losing them was a thought I couldn't bear.

'I really need to find other kids with superpowers so I can let them know about The Company, but where and how I find these kids, I have no idea,' I said to Elliot.

'Is there anyone you can think of that could have a superpower?' he asked.

'Like who?' I replied as if Elliot had asked me a dumb question, but then I started to think.

'Hey, you don't reckon Liam could have a super-power, do you? I mean, out of nowhere he suddenly becomes amazing at the high jump. Doesn't that seem a little suspicious?'

'But he did say he hadn't felt ready yet to jump higher heights,' Elliot responded.

'That's because he was trying to throw us off the scent. Can't you see? He probably doesn't want us to suspect that he has a superpower. Maybe, like me, he wants to keep it a secret.'

'But why would Liam act like he was rubbish at the high jump one day, only to show everyone how good he was the next?'

'Well, don't forget that out of the three of us, only one will get selected to take part in the county championship, and I suppose Liam wants to make sure that it's him. I wouldn't be surprised if he too could break the world record. But I bet he'll stick to jumping heights that look more achievable – you know, to avoid bringing more attention to himself.'

'So what's the plan?' said Elliot. 'Are you just gonna ask him straight out if he has a superpower? Because I have a feeling he'll say no even if he does.'

'Then maybe I'll just have to tell him about my powers. Hopefully that will encourage him to tell the truth,' I said. 'Either way, what's important is Liam knowing that he could be in danger. It wouldn't be right if I didn't let him know that.'

CHAPTER 44

I decided to find out whether Liam had a super-power during high jump practice on Wednesday. Not using my own superpowers meant I was still terrible at the high jump, and today I couldn't clear 1.28m, whereas Liam attempted and succeeded at clearing 1.64m.

'You need to give me some tips, Liam,' I said to him, as we watched Elliot flounder at his second attempt at clearing 1.30m.

'That's what Mr Jarvis is for. You should be asking him for tips,' was Liam's curt response.

'I think it's brilliant *and* inspiring how you're now jumping as high as one sixty-four compared to the heights that you used to jump,' I continued anyway.

'It's like you've got a superpower,' I added, not bothering to be subtle about it.

I did think Liam would've at least looked a little taken aback that I'd sussed out his secret, but his face didn't change at all.

'Well, if there were such a thing as superpowers, I'm sure I'd be jumping much higher than one sixty-four,' he replied as Elliot came over.

'Oh, so you don't believe in superpowers then?' I said, briefly glancing at Elliot.

'Why would I?' said Liam.

'I actually happen to think superpowers are real, and according to my aunt, when she was growing up in Delmere, there were kids who had superpowers. She even knew a boy whose powers made him super strong,' I said.

'Ha! As if you think I'm gonna believe that!' Liam sniffed.

'I'm being serious. There was also a sinister company that wanted to take the kids' powers away from them.'

'Are you sure your aunt wasn't telling you about a film she'd watched? Because superpowers aren't real, Sonny. You do know that, don't you?' said Liam, and it was blatantly clear he wasn't believing anything I was saying.

'No, it's true,' I insisted, and Elliot nodded in support.

'Are you sure you didn't bang your head on the bar, because you're chatting some real gibberish right now?' Liam scoffed.

'I've got powers!' I decided to just come out with it, which only made Liam crack up with laughter.

'Yeah, you definitely banged your head, because you've clearly lost all sense of reality!' He snickered. 'Look, if you want to be as good as me, just work on your technique, which I have to say, Sonny, does need *a lot* of work.'

Liam then went off to take a jump at 1.66m, and I was glad to see him make a mess of it, his trainers clipping the bar and making it fall.

'If you ask me, I don't think Liam has a superpower,' whispered Elliot.

'Yeah, you're probably right,' I replied.

Except there was a part of me that wasn't fully convinced that Liam was *superpower-less*, so after our practice session, I decided to do a bit more digging. Liam was one of the last boys left in the changing room, along with Parvin and Zeki.

'I'll see you tomorrow,' I said to them as I wandered out. But without them knowing, I snuck back in, hiding out of view.

They were all bragging to each other about smashing their personal bests, and to my astonishment, I finally uncovered the truth about Liam, all thanks to Zeki.

'I might not have gone over one sixty-six today, but by next week it won't be a problem,' Liam was saying. 'It really is great being the new star of the athletics team.'

'That's only because your parents have been paying for you to have private coaching,' said Zeki.

So that's why Liam had become so good!

'Oh, I wish I hadn't told you that now.' Liam sighed.

'You told us because you want to be part of the cool squad,' said Parvin. 'But I'm afraid to say, three's a crowd. Zeki and I don't need another best mate.'

'But you said I could start hanging out with you. I've had enough of everyone thinking I'm a geek, whereas you guys, you're really popular.'

I'd heard enough and walked out of the changing room, leaving Liam to carry on grovelling to Parvin and Zeki. When I saw Elliot I told him what Liam had said.

'Private coaching, eh?' he remarked as we walked out of school. 'But I suppose it does make sense of how Liam went from zero to high jump hero. At least you know now that he definitely doesn't have a superpower.'

I left Elliot at the bus stop and began my walk home, wondering if there might be other kids I knew who could have a superpower. Only there wasn't anyone I knew who was remarkable in any way. For a minute, however, I wondered if Elliot might have a superpower, seeing as he was so good at maths. He was like a human calculator and often didn't even need to use a real one. Then again, it would still take him a minute or two to solve a maths sum, so although Elliot was a genius, he wasn't a super-genius. And besides, I'm sure he would've told me by now if he had a superpower.

I also found myself thinking about Delilah. Firstly, what it would be like to share a cookie-dough ice cream with her and then I thought about the last time I was in Ice To Meet You and how she just seemed to disappear and reappear again. So maybe she could make herself invisible! Then again, maybe she had just been helping her dad put out the rubbish like she said. And *maybe* I needed to stop reading too much into things. There was every possibility that I was the only kid in Delmere with superpowers.

All of a sudden, I noticed something or should I say, *someone*. A man was walking behind me who I swear had been sitting at the bus stop across the road from where I left Elliot. He was wearing a black baseball cap that had *The Archer* stitched across it. So I guessed he was someone who worked there. But I couldn't see his face properly as his baseball cap was pulled down low. I did, however, notice he had a beard.

I stopped suddenly and carefully looked over my shoulder and weirdly the man had stopped too. He was whistling as he looked up at the sky. My heart started to thump. Cautiously, I carried on walking, crossing the road at a pedestrian crossing. When I looked over my shoulder again, the man was still behind me. The man was following me!

My heart was properly racing now.

Was the man from The Company? And was The Archer the headquarters of The Company? These were the panicked thoughts skating around my head.

As I looked back in terror, I began to run – and so did the man!

I ran past the local post office, Delmere Burger, then The Archer, but when I glanced back again, the man was nowhere to be seen. Still, I kept on running in case he was still following me. I didn't want the man seeing where I lived, so I ran straight to Fern Park, ducking behind a tree. As I looked around the park, I couldn't see the man, so he must've gone into The Archer, meaning I'd been right all along! The Archer wasn't just a health club. It *was* something more sinister, and belonged to The Company! They must've somehow found out about my powers and were now wanting to steal them from me.

I pulled out my phone, my hands shaking as I tried to turn on the flashlight. My body started to tingle, and as I held my phone out in front of me, I teleported straight to the hospital.

CHAPTER 45

I scared Dad's nurse as I appeared behind her while she was attending to him.

'Goodness me!' she said, turning round. 'You gave me such a fright. I didn't even hear the door go.'

'Sorry about that,' I apologised.

'Oh, don't worry. By the way, if you're wondering where the Power Piglet is that your brother brought in for your dad, it unfortunately flew out of the window to join all those other piglets the other day. I did try to stop it, but I'm afraid I couldn't catch it in time.'

'That's OK,' I mumbled.

'It was very bizarre, though, seeing all those piglets in the sky, but obviously there was a fault with them,' said the nurse.

I lowered my eyes for a second.

'So how's my dad doing?' I asked.

The nurse smiled delicately. 'The same. I'm sure he'll be very happy to hear your voice, so I'll leave you to spend some time with him.'

I waited until the nurse had left the room so I could tell Dad how I'd been followed. I would've texted Mum and told her too, but I knew she'd only worry if she thought some mysterious company was after me. Telling Dad this meant I'd have to finally reveal the truth about my superpowers. So I told him everything – how I could move things with my mind and how I could fly and teleport.

'The Archer must be The Company's headquarters and it looks like they know about my powers,' I explained. 'I don't want people experimenting on me. So what should I do, Dad?'

I so badly wished his eyes would open and he could answer my question.

'I have to stop them from coming after me, so I think I'm gonna have to use my powers on them,' I said, and as I thought about this some more, it felt like it was my only option. I would have to fight back!

The time for me to be a superhero was now. And even though battling villains felt like a daunting prospect,

I was ready to do it to save myself, and all the other superpowered kids out there.

When I returned home, I told Auntie Cleo about the man in the baseball cap.

'The guy was wearing The Archer baseball cap, which makes me think that's where The Company is based,' I explained.

'The Archer? I have always had my suspicions about that place, so maybe you're right, that probably is where The Company are. Oh dear, oh dear!' said Auntie Cleo as she paced round the kitchen.

'You said it could be a lab where they extract and pickle people's brains. I'm not letting any shapeshifting aliens do that to me!'

'Shapeshifting aliens?' said Auntie Cleo, wrinkling her nose. 'Look, Sonny, that stuff I told you was just a silly story.'

'But how do you know for sure?'

'Because me and my friends made it all up, that's why. It's just stories we told ourselves when we were kids.'

'Well, The Company are still out there, Auntie Cleo, and we have to stop them!'

'They'll be very dangerous people, Sonny.'

'But I have superpowers, I can fight them.'

'No, I can't allow you to put yourself at risk. There has to be another way we can tackle them,' said Auntie Cleo.

'How do you think they might've found out about my powers?'

'Er, I'm guessing they have satellites that they've been watching and listening through.'

I swallowed nervously. 'Maybe we should tell my mum.'

'No, Sonny, I think we should wait a bit before we tell her. She'll only panic, and she's already so worried about your dad.'

'Maybe we should tell the police,' I suggested.

'Yes, that does sound like the most logical thing to do, but even if The Company are based at The Archer, there's no proof out there of their actual existence. George couldn't find any info about them, and in the end he had no choice but to go on the run.'

'But I won't have to do that, will I?' I gulped.

'I honestly don't know, Sonny,' said Auntie Cleo, her face downcast. 'Running may end up being the best solution for *all* of us.'

CHAPTER 46

I was terrified at the thought that my family and I might have to go on the run and that The Company could target my family just to get at me. That was something Auntie Cleo said they could do. However, the next day she was a lot less worried – unlike me.

'I really don't want you fretting about The Company,' she said as I was leaving the house for school. 'But if you see that man in the baseball cap again, you must let me know right away. Frankly, I couldn't care less how powerful this company might be, because *I'm* willing to take the fight to them.'

'But you don't have any superpowers. How can you fight them?' I replied.

'Well, I like to think I have good negotiation

skills, which you never know, might just work.'

'On a dangerous organisation?' I responded sceptically.

'Please don't dismiss my powers of negotiation, Sonny,' said Auntie Cleo. 'Look, there was a time when I thought your mum would never forgive me for some things that were said, but I managed to win her round and have us getting along again. So if I can work things out with your mum – who's a pretty tough nut to crack, might I add – I reckon I could get this company to back off. And if not that, then I suppose I could always throw some good insults at them and see how far that gets me.' She smiled.

As I left the house, a car pulled up outside. A bald man with a beard stepped out, who looked a lot like the man in the baseball cap who'd followed me.

'Hiya,' Auntie Cleo called out to him from the door-step as he started walking up the path.

'Do you know him, Auntie Cleo?' I asked tensely, walking back behind the man.

'Yes, he's a work colleague who's come to drop off some paperwork,' she replied as the man looked over his shoulder at me.

I pushed past him and went back inside the house, slamming the door shut.

'Sonny! Why have you just done that?! That's very rude,' said Auntie Cleo.

'I think it's him, the man in the baseball cap who followed me yesterday,' I whispered.

Auntie Cleo shook her head. 'No, you're mistaken, Sonny. Mick is just an ordinary guy. I assure you he's not some villain.'

'But he has a beard like the man in the baseball cap.'

'Lots of men have beards. They are very common, you know,' said Auntie Cleo pointedly. 'Now if you don't mind, Sonny, I'd like to let him in.'

She opened the door. 'Sorry about that, Mick, please come in,' she said apologetically.

'That's all right, Cleo,' he replied.

As I walked past Mick to go back out, he gave me a stern look. Making my way to the bus stop, I tried to remember what Baseball Cap Man had looked like, but apart from the beard there hadn't been much of his face I'd been able to make out. Maybe Mick wasn't him. Auntie Cleo was sure of it, and she'd have no reason to lie.

I told Elliot about Baseball Cap Man and how I believed The Archer was really the headquarters for The Company. Plus, I told him how Auntie Cleo and me planned to fight them: her through harsh insults, and me using my telekinetic powers to hurtle everyone in The Company into outer space, which was the idea I came up with.

'Your idea does sound better than your aunt's,' Elliot judged. 'But whoever these people are, you do know they're unlikely to survive in outer space?'

'True. I really want to find out more about this company. Maybe I should sneak into The Archer again and see what I can find.'

'But what if you do sneak into The Archer and discover that it has nothing to do with The Company? You could get into huge trouble, Sonny,' said Elliot. 'Wouldn't it be better to find out for sure by doing some research on the internet or just ask someone who could know?'

'I doubt there'll be anything about The Company on the internet, and apart from my aunt I don't know anyone I could ask.'

'You could always try Mr Goodwin. I mean, he does know all there is to know about history, and he has been teaching at our school since caveman times.'

Elliot and I giggled.

'You really think Mr Goodwin would know about The Company?'

'I'm sure he's bound to know about all the supernatural stuff that went on in 1988, so you never know, he might just,' said Elliot. 'If I was you, I'd avoid telling him about your own powers, in case The Company does have listening satellites as your aunt says. They could listen in to your conversation.'

'And they could be listening in to *our* conversation right now, and previous ones!' I said, slapping my forehead.

I felt like a right idiot.

'So we'll just have to speak in code from now on,' said Elliot. 'Instead of calling it a superpower, you could call it—'

'Smoky bacon!' I exclaimed. 'To quote one of my dad's phrases.'

'Yeah!' Elliot whispered. 'So, if I ask you if you've eaten any smoky bacon today, what I really mean is, have you used your superpowers? So, have you eaten any smoky bacon?'

'Yeah, when I was brushing my teeth.'

Elliot scrunched his face. 'Actually, that does sound kinda weird, but it should be enough to prevent The Company from understanding what we're talking about, which is what we want.'

Later on, after our history lesson, Elliot and I tried to see if we could discover anything more about The Company by asking Mr Goodwin.

'Elliot and I would like to learn more about the history of Delmere, sir, particularly the year 1988,' I began. 'My aunt, who grew up in Delmere, told me there were several strange occurrences that year, like a cat that was found frozen in ice and a month of blackouts.'

'You want to know about 1988?' said Mr Goodwin, his face looking rather impressed. 'Well, it's good to see that you're taking an interest in local history. So, what can I tell you about that year?' he continued, tapping his chin. 'Well, I'd not long been a teacher at this school, and yes, I do recall hearing about some strange incidences. I certainly remember the blackouts, that's for sure! I almost broke my elbow one night trying to find my torch. I also remember hearing about the cat, and about a cherry blossom tree on Duncan Avenue that somehow blossomed overnight during winter. No one seemed to be able to work out why that tree and no others on the road was able to blossom so quickly and out of season.'

'So you've heard about the Delmere Magic then?' I said.

'Oh, you already know about that, do you?'

'Yeah, my aunt mentioned it to me.'

Mr Goodwin rolled his eyes. 'It's a load of old hogwash if you ask me. Only conspiracy theorist types believe there's some magical force lying within this town … not that I'm suggesting your aunt is a conspiracy theorist.'

'She didn't actually tell me much about the Delmere Magic, like how it all started. Would you know, Mr Goodwin?'

'Ah, well, it supposedly dates back thousands of

years, and they say this magical force has been keeping a mythical soul-eating creature at bay called the Vellibog.'

'Wow,' I said, my eyes widening.

'And it's believed that for centuries this *magic* has caused children in Delmere to develop powers.'

'Do you think this creature still exists, sir?' asked Elliot.

'For a start, I don't believe there is any creature, but apparently it dwells in another world that exists right next to ours where there's no such thing as time, and there's no light, and it's as cold as anything.'

Hearing this suddenly made a terrifying thought burst into my mind – was this other world The Stuck Place?

I shared a glance with Elliot, and by the look on his face, he was thinking the same thing.

Could I have been somewhere where there was a soul-eating monster? I shuddered at the thought.

'So what kind of powers did the kids develop?' I asked, my voice shaking slightly as I wondered if this Vellibog creature had been nearby all those times I'd found myself in The Stuck Place.

'It's like the superpowers you see in movies,' said Mr Goodwin. 'Some people reckoned that a child froze the cat, and I've heard how decades before that, in the 1950s, there were rumours about a child being a real-life

Doctor Dolittle who could talk to the animals, and everywhere she went, the local wildlife would follow. Though I expect the child was probably carrying food in her pocket. Trust me, the Delmere Magic and the Vellibog are nothing but urban legend nonsense! It's not rooted in any historical fact,' he concluded, 'and as a historian, I only deal with the facts.'

But I was still really fascinated by what Mr Goodwin was telling us.

'So did some people believe a kid with superpowers made that tree blossom?' I asked.

'Yes, exactly that. So I guess this child would've had the ability to manipulate Mother Nature.'

'Did you ever hear of, erm, a company that might've, erm, wanted to steal those children's powers?' I asked tentatively.

Mr Goodwin had a think, but then started shaking his head. 'No, I don't remember hearing of such a company, but that was probably another tale the conspiracy theorists were putting out there.'

'Do you know much about The Archer, sir?' asked Elliot.

'You mean the gym, health-club place?'

Elliot nodded. 'Some people reckon it isn't really a health club.'

'Do they? Well, I know it was once a button factory

but other than that, I don't know much about the place,' said Mr Goodwin. 'The two of you might think this town is remarkable in some way but trust me, it isn't – though Delmere *was* once home to one of the first tea shops to ever open in this country. It's now an ice-cream parlour.'

'It's Ice To Meet You,' I said.

'I beg your pardon?' Mr Goodwin replied.

'That's the name of the ice-cream parlour. Ice To Meet You.'

'Oh, is it?' He cleared his throat awkwardly. 'I should know that, shouldn't I, being a historian? But unfortunately, I don't like ice cream,' said Mr Goodwin, which to me was more surprising than hearing about the Vellibog – because who doesn't like ice cream?

More importantly, it was so frustrating that I'd got no further in finding out more about The Company. I also had ice cream on the brain from all the talk about Ice To Meet You, so after school, Elliot and I stopped by the parlour.

'I really think the other world Mr Goodwin was talking about is The Stuck Place, especially when he said how cold and dark it was. And like I said, time is all weird there,' I said to Elliot. 'But it scares me to think there might be some dreadful creature living there that could've eaten my soul!'

'Do you think you might've seen this creature or heard it?' asked Elliot.

I shook my head.

'I've just had a thought,' I said. 'What if the issues I've had with teleporting have something to do with the Vellibog? Maybe it was drawing me into The Stuck Place so it could capture me because it wanted my soul and my powers. And maybe it doesn't like bright lights, which is why I've been able to escape quickly when my phone's flashlight is on.' I held my breath. 'I'm just glad I have been able to escape.'

'I think you might be worrying about nothing, Sonny. Mr Goodwin did say the Vellibog is just an urban legend,' said Elliot.

'Do you reckon there's a way the Vellibog could get out?'

'Well, if it does really exist, seeing as it hasn't managed to get out in thousands of years, I doubt that it can,' said Elliot. 'Anyway, it's a shame Mr Goodwin didn't know about The Company. But it was very interesting when he was talking about those kids' smoky bacon.'

'What smoky bacon?' I said, then instantly remembered it was our code word. 'Oh right, *that* smoky bacon. Yeah, I'm beginning to think it's true that some kid used their smoky bacon to freeze the cat, even if Mr Goodwin doesn't believe it. And if the Delmere Magic definitely is real, then maybe that's how I got my smoky bacon, just like my Auntie Cleo reckons.'

After we'd finished our ice creams, it was time for me to head home, and as I waved goodbye to Elliot, that's when I saw him – BASEBALL CAP MAN, standing on the other side of the road! I suddenly panicked, and even if I'd wanted to use my powers to hurl him to the moon, I couldn't think! Instead I bolted, running straight into a clothes shop.

Here was I, wanting to be superhero but acting like a big scaredy-cat. I mean, you wouldn't catch Batman hiding behind a rail of T-shirts.

'Can I help you, young man?' said a shop assistant, coming over to me.

'Um ... um ...'

'Is there something you wish to buy?' she asked.

I looked around the shop awkwardly. It was a women's fashion shop that sold the kind of clothes that would appeal more to someone like Mrs Armstrong than, say, someone like my mum, or someone 'with any real taste', which was what my mum had said once when we were walking past the shop.

'No, there's nothing I want to buy,' I replied, then hastily walked out. I looked around to check if I could see the man, and thankfully he was nowhere in sight. I breathed a HUGE sigh of relief, but it didn't stop me from feeling any less worried, and I quickly ran home.

The second I got in, I called out to Auntie Cleo so I could tell her about the man. But I was greeted by Ramona and Oscar, who came running out into the hall, throwing their arms around me as if they'd never been more pleased to see me.

'Whoa, what's going on? What are you so excited about?'

'It's Dad!' Ramona exclaimed. 'He's woken up!'

CHAPTER 47

I'd never been more ecstatic in my whole life than I was at hearing that Dad had woken up. Auntie Cleo on the other hand didn't seem to share my joy. She was sitting in the living room with her arms folded, staring into space.

'Ramona just told me the good news about Dad,' I said to her.

'Yes, the hospital called a short while ago to tell us,' she replied in a wistful tone.

I know she and Dad weren't exactly best buddies, but I thought she could've at least looked a little chuffed that he was awake.

'Can we go and see him?' I asked.

'Um, no, I don't think that's a good idea, Sonny. I don't think he's been awake for that long and he's probably feeling very tired, plus he might not be that responsive,' said Auntie Cleo.

'But he'll be happy to see us, and I've really missed him.'

'Me too. Let's go and see him now,' said Oscar.

'No!' said Auntie Cleo tersely. 'You can go tomorrow, not today.'

I didn't want to wait until tomorrow, and as I marched off to the kitchen, I found myself feeling mega cross that Auntie Cleo wouldn't let us see Dad. As I took a packet of crisps from the cupboard, I deliberately banged the cupboard door hard. Auntie Cleo came in, closing the kitchen door behind her.

'Why are you trying to stop us from seeing our dad?' I demanded to know.

'I'm not. I'm just concerned that he might not be up to seeing visitors just yet,' she whispered.

'But we've been visiting him since he went into hospital. Plus, I want to tell him about my superpowers again, and about The Company, in case he didn't hear what I was saying when he was in the coma,' I said, munching on a crisp.

'You really shouldn't have told him, Sonny, and you mustn't tell him again!' snapped Auntie Cleo, then exhaled a breath. 'I'm sorry. Just try and look at it from your dad's perspective. He's still not very well, and him hearing that some ghastly company is after you could cause him a great deal of stress. And you do want to see your dad get better, don't you?'

I considered this for a moment. I didn't want my dad to be any more unwell, but I still needed to see him.

'I saw the man in the baseball cap again,' I said to Auntie Cleo.

'You did?!' she said, looking horrified. 'Oh gosh! Why can't this company just leave you alone?!'

'Well, right now I don't want to think about them. I just want to see my dad!' I put down the packet of crisps and took out my phone. I turned on the flashlight.

'What are you doing?' said Auntie Cleo.

'I'm going to the hospital,' I replied, and as my arms and legs began to tingle, I teleported myself out of the kitchen right in front of her.

CHAPTER 48

There was no one but Dad in his room as I emerged inside it. Dad still had his eyes closed, and at first I wondered if it was a lie that he'd woken up.

I went over to the bed.

'*Dad!* Dad, can you hear me?' I whispered.

Slowly Dad's eyes began to open.

'S-S-Sonny. Is that you?' he stuttered, his voice all croaky.

'Dad!' I said, feeling a rush of relief. I gently squeezed his hand. 'Do you know where you are, Dad?'

'The h-h-hospital.'

'So you remember the accident then?' I said, but then wished that I hadn't, as a pained expression appeared on Dad's face.

'We've so missed having you around, but we've been visiting you lots,' I said.

'Oscar ... Ramona,' he murmured weakly.

'They're at home, they wanted to come but ... they're going to come tomorrow,' I said. 'We'd chat to you loads when we'd come and visit. Could you hear what we were saying?'

'No,' Dad mumbled.

'Oh. Well, when I was last here, I told you about something I've discovered about myself.'

'Huh?'

I so badly wanted to tell Dad about my superpowers, but he looked so confused.

'It's nothing,' I replied. I paused for a moment. 'Auntie Cleo's been looking after us.'

'*Cleo*,' murmured Dad.

'Yeah, she's been looking after us while Mum's working. Mum is still in Jordan.'

'I don't like that woman,' said Dad, his face grimacing but with difficulty.

'I think you'll find she's not the same person you remember. She's much nicer now,' I said, despite my recent frustration with Auntie Cleo.

Dad tried to shake his head. 'No, Cleo's not nice. She's a b-b-bad person. I don't trust her, and I don't w-w-want her in our home. I want to speak to your mum.'

'She might be busy, so I don't know if she'll pick up, but I can give her a call.'

I called Mum's mobile, and luckily, after a few rings, she picked up.

'Hi, Mum, it's Sonny. I'm at the hospital with Dad—'

'Hello, sweetheart,' she replied cheerfully. 'Yes, I know he's woken up. The hospital called earlier.'

'He wants to speak to you.'

I put my phone on speaker and put it on Dad's chest.

'Hello, Bev,' said Dad.

'Oh, darling, I can't tell you how happy I am that you're awake,' said Mum, her voice full of emotion.

Dad looked at me.

'I just want a f-f-few minutes with your mum, in private.'

'OK, Dad. I'll be back in a bit,' I said, then left the room and the ward.

To pass the time, I mooched up and down a corridor, thinking about what Dad had said about Auntie Cleo.

I knew she'd said some horrible things about him in the past, but was she really as bad as Dad was making out? And why did he say he didn't trust her?

After ten minutes I went back to Dad's room, and it looked like his conversation had already ended. I took back my phone.

Dad reached for my hand.

'You mustn't trust your Auntie Cleo,' he said.

'Why not?'

'She w-w-wanted me and your mother to split up, as well as other stuff,' he muttered.

'I know you don't like Auntie Cleo, Dad, but I think I need *her* to tell me what she's done wrong,' I said, though my words came out in a muddle. I was feeling confused now. 'I'm going to go, Dad, but I promise I'll visit you again soon,' I told him.

He gave me a tiny smile and I kissed his cheek and walked out. Standing out of view beside a vending machine, I took out my phone and turned on the flashlight. My body went all tingly and I teleported back home, quietly appearing behind Auntie Cleo, who was sitting at the kitchen table. She was on her phone.

'I promise you the plan is not ruined, so nothing changes, OK?' she was saying. 'Everything's coming together, trust me.'

She looked over her shoulder, and jumped when she saw me.

'Sonny! Oh, thank goodness you're back!' she said, quickly putting her mobile in her lap.

'Who were you talking to?'

'Oh, just my boss at work. There was some stuff I needed to confirm with her. Were you standing there for long?'

I shook my head.

'By the way, Ramona and Oscar think you're helping out Mrs Armstrong. I had to come up with something to explain how you'd suddenly disappeared from the house. So they think you climbed over the fence to help her sort out her computer.'

I didn't respond and instead looked at Auntie Cleo guardedly.

'So did you manage to see your dad in the hospital?' she asked.

I nodded.

'Was he responsive?'

'Yep.'

'You didn't tell your dad about The Company or about your superpowers, did you? I'd hate to think you've left Adam feeling overwhelmed, because it would be pretty shocking news for him.'

'I didn't tell him, but he told me something.'

'What did he say?'

I narrowed my eyes at her. 'He said I shouldn't trust you. So tell me, why would he say that?'

Auntie Cleo shrugged her shoulders. 'I have no idea, Sonny. But he has just woken up from a coma, so I expect he's feeling all sorts of emotions right now. Or maybe he's still angry with me from when I had that falling-out with your mum the last Christmas I was here. You were much younger then, so you probably wouldn't remember—'

'I do actually. I remember bits, and I particularly remember you calling my dad a failure.'

'That was just something I said in the heat of the moment,' said Auntie Cleo quietly. 'But tomorrow, when I see your dad, I'll apologise properly, OK?'

I slowly nodded, but for the rest of the evening, Dad's words lingered inside my head, and I couldn't help wondering: should I really trust Auntie Cleo?

'I'm sorry if I seemed like I was stopping you from seeing your dad yesterday,' said Auntie Cleo as I was getting ready to leave for school the next morning. 'I was just worried he might not have been ready for visitors. And I know he might still think ill of me, but I really do want to make amends.'

Seeing Auntie Cleo being so apologetic made me feel guilty for doubting that I could trust her. Maybe she was right: my dad was just feeling a bit emotional, so that's why he said those things about her.

I made my way to the bus stop and waited for Elliot.

'That's fantastic news!' Elliot smiled when I told him about my dad coming out of his coma.

'I'm just looking forward to him coming home now,' I said as we walked to school. I also told Elliot about seeing the man from The Company again.

'I wanted to use my super ... I mean smoky bacon on him, but I was too scared,' I told him.

'Well, if you see him again, you're going to have to be much braver, Sonny.'

'I know. All the superheroes I read about in my comics are always so brave. I'd love to be like them, but I don't know how.' I frowned.

'Yes, you do. I mean, just look how you coped with your dad being in a coma and your mum being away. That's well brave, if you ask me.'

I nodded reluctantly.

'There is one way, you know, you could test out your bravery without even having to use your smoky bacon,' said Elliot.

'What?'

Elliot stopped in his tracks and pointed towards the east entrance to school.

'You can take on Milo Allerton.'

I looked at Elliot as if he'd lost his mind.

'Are you serious?' I spluttered.

There was no way I could take on Milo! Even that time when I made Kayla's phone fall out of his hand, that wasn't bravery I'd been feeling – it was just anger.

'Look, if you can stand up to him, then you can stand up to anyone,' said Elliot. 'Anyways, haven't you just about had enough of him acting like he owns this school?'

I had had enough of Milo, though I knew I'd need bravery the size of a mountain to take him on. I suppose I didn't have that much to lose; well, apart from my legs maybe.

My stomach clenched but I found myself nodding at Elliot before I tentatively began walking towards the east entrance. And as I stood at the top of it, I could see that Milo and his goons were already on standby, their chewing-gum weaponry in the palms of their hands, waiting to strike any Year Seven who dared to tread this forbidden footpath.

I tried thinking of what I could say to Milo. Perhaps I could come out with some quality insults, or I could just say to him that he had no right to tell anyone what to do.

And so, I stepped forward.

CHAPTER 49

As soon as my foot touched the sacred path, that was enough for Milo and his gang to spring into action. I swiftly shielded my face with my rucksack as missile after missile came shooting at me. But I continued to plough forward.

'Get off our path!' Milo spat.

'No, I'm not going to!' I somehow found the courage to say, despite having a big lump in my throat.

It felt like there were dozens and dozens of chewing-gum missiles coming towards me.

PLINK, PLINK, PLINK, THWACK!!!

One hit my ear.

It did sting, but only a teeny bit. Then suddenly there was a ceasefire, or I guess they'd run out of chewing gum. I lowered my rucksack, realising it was now time for me to face down Milo.

'WHAT DO YOU THINK YOU'RE DOING, YEAR SEVEN?!' he exploded.

'I'M NOT GOING TO LET YOU BULLY ME, THAT'S WHAT I'M DOING!' I roared back. I really wasn't sure where I was finding all this confidence from.

Milo looked taken aback. It was probably the first time anyone had dared to stand up to him.

'You've got your own entrance! We don't want you down here!' he said, although his voice shook a little.

'This entrance belongs to everyone, and us Year Sevens should be able to go wherever we like,' I said, as Elliot slowly came up the path along with a group of Year Sevens and kids from other years. They all began to crowd around.

'You don't own this school, Milo, or this path!' I yelled.

'That's right, you tell him!' I heard a voice say, and when I looked at the person, I saw it was Delilah and she threw me an encouraging smile.

'We're fed up with you and your mates thinking you can tell us what to do,' I said, as kids started to whoop and clap in support. 'But it ends today! All Year Sevens will be free to use this entrance and there won't be a single thing you'll be able to do about it!'

Strangely, Milo was completely lost for words and kept blinking slowly like one of Ramona's old baby dolls when the batteries are dying.

'Is that right?' his friend Omar answered for him.

'YEAH!' I replied boldly, my arms crossed as I continued glaring at Milo.

Omar turned to his friend. 'Milo, are you just gonna let him speak to you like that?'

Milo glanced back at Omar, and suddenly it was as if it had finally dawned on him that he was being totally shown up by a Year Seven.

The next thing I knew, he was shoving me, and without thinking I shoved him right back, using all the strength I had, which made Milo almost fall backwards. Then Milo took a swing at me, but I instantly ducked. He tried swinging at me a second and a third time, but my reflexes were sharp, and I managed to duck again.

'MILO ALLERTON! WHAT ON EARTH DO YOU THINK YOU'RE DOING?!' The voice of Mrs Somerville boomed like a loudspeaker.

Everyone gasped as she marched fiercely towards us.

'He's trying to beat up Sonny, miss,' said a voice from the crowd, which made her shake her head in outrage.

'Milo, Aiden, Omar, Charlie, my office, now!' she commanded.

With sullen faces, Milo and his friends followed as everyone cheered and began to congratulate me.

'That was awesome how you handled Milo!' said Liam, patting me on the back.

'You were so brave, Sonny,' said both Delilah and Holly together.

I was certainly feeling brave and full of confidence, which was just what I needed to help me on my way to becoming a superhero.

'It was well wicked the way you were ducking Milo's punches,' said Zeki. 'So I guess if you ever get fed up with the high jump, you could always take up boxing.'

Heaps of other kids congratulated me too, even Parvin.

'Well done,' he said simply, holding out his hand for me to shake.

'Thanks,' I replied, and we exchanged a smile.

It felt great knowing I'd given Milo a dressing-down, or at least left Mrs Somerville to do that. And for the first time ever, I was one of the popular kids! Throughout the day more kids came up to me, many of whom I didn't even know.

'Is it true you once battled a six-foot python?' said a boy called Brett, who was in another Year Seven form. I found out it was Elliot who started that crazy rumour as a way of bigging me up to the max.

I had to of course tell Brett that I hadn't.

'Is it true that you're super smart at maths?' asked a Year Eight girl called Naomi.

Elliot was also responsible for that rumour, despite knowing full well that *he's* the maths whizz, not me. All in all, everyone was just pleased that Milo and his friends had got their comeuppance.

I did have to go and speak to Mrs Somerville, however, and give my side of the story on what had happened. I also told her how Milo and his friends had banned Year Sevens from using the east entrance, which she wasn't happy about whatsoever.

But overall, it had turned out to be a brilliant day, and the best thing about it and my new-found fame was that Delilah said I could have a free ice cream the next time I was in Ice To Meet You. Hearing this even topped the news that Milo and his gang were going to be excluded. I was still on a high when I got home, but as I came in, I was surprised to see Auntie Cleo's suitcases in the hall.

'Are you leaving?' I asked as she took her jacket off the coat hook.

'I'm afraid so, Sonny,' she replied with a frown. 'I've had a fabulous job offer abroad which I simply couldn't refuse. So I'll be leaving very shortly.'

'Do Ramona and Oscar know that you're leaving?' I

asked, a bit stunned that Auntie Cleo was going so soon. 'Where are they?'

'Yes, they do know, and right now they're playing over at Blessing's house. But don't worry, Mrs Armstrong has offered to take care of you all. Now that your dad's awake, I expect your mum will be home in the next few days,' said Auntie Cleo. 'Though, there is something I'm going to need your help with before I leave.'

'What is it?'

Just then the doorbell rang.

'Would you mind getting that, Sonny? I just need to grab something,' said Auntie Cleo, and sprinted up the stairs.

I opened the door. It was Auntie Cleo's work colleague Mick.

'Hello,' I said as I let him in.

Mick just nodded.

'My aunt's just looking for something. She's got a new job abroad. Did you know that?'

He nodded again but didn't speak.

'Mick, you're here!' said Auntie Cleo, coming back down the stairs. She waved her passport. 'I almost forgot this.'

'And I almost forgot this,' said Mick, and from his jacket he pulled out a baseball cap.

He put it over his head and pulled it down low as he stared directly at me, a menacing smile on his lips.

My face dropped in horror. Mick *was* Baseball Cap Man!

'It's *him*, Auntie Cleo!' I gasped, as all the bravery I'd felt earlier vanished in a heartbeat. And once again I felt too scared to even attempt to use my superpowers on him. 'He's the man from The Company!'

'Who, Mick?' said Auntie Cleo, looking at him quizzically.

'Yeah,' I uttered.

'Oh, what am I like,' said Auntie Cleo, shaking her head. 'I really should've properly introduced you both.' She went up to Mick and rested her hands on his shoulder. 'Mick, meet Sonny, my stupendous nephew.'

CHAPTER 50

'It's a pleasure to formally meet you, Sonny.' Mick grinned as my eyes darted between him and Auntie Cleo in HUMONGOUS shock. I felt like an elephant had landed on my head.

'Y-y-you've been f-f-following me,' I said, struggling to get my words out.

Auntie Cleo rolled her eyes. 'I'd call it keeping an eye on you, which I asked this amazing boyfriend of mine to do.'

'He's your boyfriend!' I muttered, feeling even more shocked and confused as Auntie Cleo threw me a cruel smile.

It was like her whole personality had changed, with her going from being caring and loving one minute to truly foul the next.

I gawped at her in disbelief. 'But why was he following me?'

'Because you have very special abilities, Sonny. We needed to know if you were using them in public. After all, we really can't afford for you to bring attention to yourself,' said Auntie Cleo, a spiteful expression on her face.

'Are you both from The Company?' I said, which made Auntie Cleo cackle with laughter.

'There is no company, Sonny,' she said, tossing her head to one side. 'I made it all up, along with making up that Mick was my work colleague.'

I blinked. 'But if there isn't a company, then what is The Archer?'

'It's a health club, Sonny, trust me. Mick only has a baseball cap because he stole it when he snuck in one day and broke into a few lockers. You managed to get your hands on quite a bit of cash, didn't you, Mick?'

'I sure did,' he replied with a grin.

'I don't understand,' I said bewilderedly.

I looked at Mick again, then at Auntie Cleo.

'I want to know what's going on!' I demanded.

'I intend to tell you everything. As I said, there's something I'd like your help with,' said Auntie Cleo, motioning me towards the living room.

Mick sat down in one of the armchairs, his mean

eyes fixed on me, while Auntie Cleo perched on the armrest. But I didn't sit down.

'You probably don't realise this, Sonny, but your powers could be put to some really good use,' Auntie Cleo began.

'W-w-what do you mean?' I stammered.

'Well, they could make me, Mick *and* yourself incredibly rich. We could all be billionaires, maybe even trillionaires!' she exclaimed. 'Just think about it: all that money lying in safes, vaults, tills, wallets and piggy banks all over the world, and you have the power to make it all appear right in front of us instantly!'

I couldn't believe what Auntie Cleo was saying as I looked at her, totally staggered.

'So, that's what we need your help with, Sonny. We need you to use your powers to make that money appear right now. So just like how you made all the Power Piglets float away, this time think about all the money in the world appearing here in this living room.'

'I think you're best off just making it a few million. Any more and this house will probably burst!' Mick said, then hooted with laughter.

I shook my head hard. 'No, I'm not a thief!'

'But we are!' said Mick, still laughing.

'*Part-time* thieves, Mick,' Auntie Cleo corrected him, before looking at me again.

Dad was right, Auntie Cleo really was a bad person and someone I should never have trusted, and it was clear that all the kindness she'd shown was all fake.

'The thought of you and your siblings having super-powers was the only reason why I came here in the first place,' she said.

'So you'd planned this all along?' I muttered.

Then it struck me: the secret conversations Auntie Cleo was having on the phone, talking about plans and things coming together. That wasn't her boss she was speaking to – that was Mick!

'At first I didn't know you had superpowers, but I'd always had a feeling that the Delmere Magic hadn't gone away. So when I read on social media there was a freak tornado in Ocean View, I was sure there were still kids in this county gaining superpowers. And when your mum called to tell me about your dad's foolish accident, of course I jumped at the chance to come and look after you kids as it provided me with the perfect opportunity to find out if any of you had superpowers. And, Sonny, you do – which is brilliant!'

I shot her a glowering look as something else suddenly dawned on me. 'The reason why you didn't want me to tell my dad about The Company was in case he worked out your criminal plan! But I don't get why you went to all those lengths to make me think there were people after me.'

'It's called mind games,' said Mick, tapping his forehead, while Auntie Cleo just shrugged, unbothered.

'Well, I'm not going to let you play with my mind any longer! And I'm not doing anything you tell me to!' I said to Auntie Cleo.

'Look, we really don't have time to hang about,' said Mick. 'We've got a flight to Venezuela to catch, so just get us that money now!'

'No! I'm not going to steal any money!' I responded fearlessly.

'Yes, you are,' said Auntie Cleo, her voice impatient. 'Because if you don't, we'll make sure the whole world finds out about your superpowers, and I expect there really are some evil organisations out there who'd be very happy to turn you into a lab rat. That person I knew, George, remained convinced a company was after her.'

'*Her*? I thought you said George was a boy.'

'Oops, my mistake,' said Auntie Cleo mockingly. 'George is actually short for Georgina, and she wasn't just some kid in my class. She was my best friend – that was, until she decided not to do as I asked.'

'What happened to her?! What did you do?!'

'It should've been me who got a superpower, not gormless George!' Auntie Cleo snapped. 'George was actually terrified of her power because she couldn't even do simple things like throw a ball without causing severe damage to something or someone.'

'What did you do?' I repeated.

Auntie Cleo sighed. 'All I wanted was for her to steal a few clothes from a shop. She didn't even need to use her superpower. But she refused, so I got my revenge.'

'How?'

Auntie Cleo stood up. 'This had all happened around the same time George was approached by a woman who told her she knew about her superpower, which got George all in a panic. So all *I* did was make George think that the woman was from a shady company who were intent on stealing her power. I managed to scare George so much that she and her mum left Delmere.'

'By God, Cleo, you're a clever woman!' said Mick.

Auntie Cleo took a bow.

'No, she's not! She's a TERRIBLE woman!' I said, as Auntie Cleo threw me another cruel smile.

'Years later, I really did see George in Tenerife, and I didn't lie when I said she told me that her superpower disappeared when she turned eighteen,' said Auntie Cleo. 'This means yours will go as well, Sonny. So you have to make the most of it now! All the money in the world could be yours and ours!'

'I've already told you, I'm not using my powers to steal money!'

'But can't you see? You'll not only be helping us but also your mum and dad. Every one of us could be stinking rich!'

'I'm not going to do it, so just GO AWAY!' I thundered, and levitated up until I was looming over them. As my brain buzzed fiercely, with my mind I sent a cup and saucer that were on the coffee table whizzing into the wall. They smashed into pieces. Both Auntie Cleo and Mick looked scared.

'Easy now, kid. Just stay calm,' said Mick, leaping out of the chair.

Just then the front door opened.

'Kids!' a voice called out.

It was Mum. And it was such a relief to hear her voice.

'Mum! I'm in the living room.'

She came in, her face dropping in astonishment at me levitating in the air.

'Oh, my God! How did you get up there, Sonny?!' she exclaimed.

'I was going to tell you, Mum. I, erm, kind of have superpowers,' I said, lowering myself back down.

Mum looked in complete shock. 'S-s-superpowers! How? What?'

She looked at Auntie Cleo and Mick, who were staring back icily, then looked at me again.

'What's going on?' she asked.

'Auntie Cleo and her boyfriend are trying to get me to use my powers to steal money.'

'They're trying to get you to do *what*?!' Mum barked, her eyes flashing at Auntie Cleo. 'Well, it's a good thing I'm back. Don't worry, Sonny, I'll deal with my sister.'

With her arms folded, Mum walked up to Auntie Cleo.

'Adam revealed something very interesting when I spoke to him yesterday. It's about the last time you were here, that Christmas.' Mum shook her head at her. 'He told me how he caught you with my chequebook trying to write out a cheque to yourself and signing it in my name! But he chose not to tell me after you promised that you wouldn't step foot in this house ever again.'

'I only wanted a few hundred quid. I really don't see what the big deal was,' said Auntie Cleo stiffly.

Mum and I looked at Auntie Cleo in disgust.

'I also realise now that you deliberately started the row we had about Adam *after* you were caught trying to steal from me, because you knew I'd get upset arguing with you and therefore ask you to leave. But I guess you preferred that over coming clean that you were actually trying to steal from me. How could you, Cleo?' Mum threw her arms up in the air. 'I guess it was an easy escape for you, and all this time my lovely husband was shielding me from the truth. But like I did back then, I'm going to tell you once and once only to GET OUT OF MY HOUSE!'

'We're not going anywhere until Sonny gets us our money!' said Auntie Cleo as Mick suddenly lunged towards me – but Mum blocked him.

'Don't worry, Mum, I'll take care of this,' I said and as my mind began to buzz, the sofa shot out in front of Mick, pushing both him and Auntie Cleo back against the wall.

Mick tried to push the sofa off of them, but it wouldn't budge.

'We're trapped!' said Auntie Cleo.

'Good!' said Mum then kissed my forehead. 'Well done, Sonny.'

'Thanks!' I beamed.

CHAPTER 51

'I've got a good mind to call the police right now, Cleo,' said my mum angrily. 'However, there is an alternative you might wish to consider.'

'And what might that be?' said Auntie Cleo.

'That you promise to never step foot in Delmere again, and never come near me and my family ever.'

Auntie Cleo took only a second to think about this.

'I'll take the alternative. We were planning to go to Venezuela anyway, so none of you will have to worry about seeing the two of us again.'

'And you swear you won't come back?' I said.

'Oh, I have no interest in coming back here, believe me,' said Auntie Cleo.

'Well, to make sure, I'll take you to Venezuela myself. I'll teleport us there,' I said.

'Teleport? But you said that it doesn't always work properly,' Auntie Cleo muttered hesitantly.

'Is that true?' said Mum. 'Because, Sonny, I'm not sure I want you teleporting anywhere if that's the case. Are you certain it's going to work?'

'Yeah, Mum, it'll be all right, don't worry. And teleporting is really quick, so I'll be back before you know it,' I told her.

I'd never teleported with anyone before, or to another country, but I believed it would work.

My powers were still keeping Auntie Cleo and Mick pinned to the wall, and as I switched on my phone's flashlight, with my mind I moved the sofa away from them.

'You really will take us to Venezuela, won't you, and not to some planet in space?' said Auntie Cleo as she nervously held on to Mick's hand.

'Yes, we're going to Venezuela,' I said, taking hold of Auntie Cleo's other hand.

'On the bright side, I suppose it does beat spending several hours on a plane,' said Mick, trying to see the bright side of things even though it was obvious he was terrified. 'But please just make sure we get there in one piece.'

A moment later we were all gone. The first thing I noticed as we reappeared were the high trees, the heat, the pungent smell of wildlife, and the countless plants sprouting up from the ground with big thick leaves.

'Are you sure this definitely is Venezuela?' said Auntie Cleo uneasily.

'Yes. We're in the jungle,' I replied, as birds flew above us, their chirruping echoing all around.

Just before we'd teleported, I'd imagined in my head this same Venezuelan jungle, which had been a photo in one of my geography books. It felt amazing to be here, but a little unnerving too, as I was sure I could hear the hissing of a snake nearby. Auntie Cleo and Mick definitely heard it because their eyes immediately widened in alarm.

'How are we supposed to find our way out of here?' said Mick anxiously.

I shrugged. 'That's your problem, not mine.'

Suddenly Mick let out a shriek as a butterfly flew into his face. I stifled a giggle.

'Let's not worry too much, Mick. Perhaps, we can see it as a little adventure,' said Auntie Cleo, but her voice sounded doubtful.

She looked at me. 'I guess this is the last time you'll see me, Sonny.'

'And I can't tell you how glad I am about that. See ya!' was all I had to say before I teleported myself back home, and as soon as I reappeared, Mum threw her arms around me.

'Oh, thank goodness you're back safe,' she said. 'Did you teleport OK? Did you take them to Venezuela?'

'Yeah, to the jungle,' I replied.

'That will be an interesting experience for them, especially as Cleo has never been the outdoorsy type.' Mum giggled. 'But I must say, I still can't quite believe you have superpowers. It's the most phenomenal thing I've ever heard! You really are our Stupendous Sonny!'

'I've wanted to tell you and Dad for ages.'

'Well, I'm all ears! I'm back home now for good,' said Mum. 'As your dad's awake, I want to spend as much time with him as I can, and spend lots of time with you, Ramona and Oscar. I know I've got a lot of making up to do for not being here when your dad had his accident and not being here to take care of you. I hope you can forgive me, Sonny.'

I nodded my head as Mum put her arm around me. 'I never should've left you with Cleo. I only wish I'd known sooner just how despicable she is.'

'It's OK, Mum. I'm just happy you're home, and I can't wait for Dad to come home too!'

Later that evening, I texted Elliot to tell him all about my aunt and her partner in crime, and he texted back three *OMG*s, then phoned me afterwards to get the full lowdown on what had happened. He reckoned I was definitely worthy of calling myself a superhero for saving the world from global bankruptcy, which made me feel pretty chuffed. Never in a billion years, though, would I have helped Auntie Cleo get her hands on a single banknote. Most of all, I was pleased that I'd never have to set eyes on her or Mick again. Plus, at last I really did feel like a superhero.

CHAPTER 52

I told Dad about my superpowers when we all went to see him with Mum the next day, but before that, I told Ramona and Oscar *again*, which had them cracking up with laughter. Not that their laughter lasted long once I'd shown them what I could do, and they were mightily impressed, especially when I took each of them flying around the garden. And they gasped and went *wheeeeeee!* when I used my telekinetic powers to rearrange the furniture with them seated on it. Ramona said it was like being on the dodgems at a funfair.

Oscar was left captivated when, with my mind, I built a tower super fast with his Lego and made his four Power Piglets pile on top of each other like a stunt display team and had them zooming around the house on his toy dump truck.

And both my brother and sister enjoyed my game of 'Guess Where?', which involved me teleporting myself to different parts of the house and them having to come and find me. Which I suppose was my version of hide-and-seek.

'There's something I've been meaning to tell you for a while,' I said to Dad as he sat up in his hospital bed.

It was just me and him in the room. Mum had stepped out with Ramona and Oscar so I could speak to Dad in private.

'What is it, Sonny?' he replied.

'It's something that's pretty amazing.'

'Well, tell me then,' he pressed.

I took a breath. 'I have superpowers.'

Dad gave me an inquisitive look for a moment, then he started to laugh.

'That has to be the funniest thing I've heard in a long time,' he said, but his laughing quickly descended into coughs. I fetched him some water and he drank it down.

'I'm OK,' said Dad, handing me back the beaker. 'But I know what this is. You want to convince me that I've woken up in the year 2050 or whatever, and want to make out that it wasn't a coma I was in, but a cryonic vessel where I lay frozen until someone came and thawed me out.' He folded his arms. 'So tell me, has the government been taken over by space aliens? Is all of mankind living on Martian food? Have pigs developed wings so they can fly? And I take it nobody ages, which would explain why you still look like a twelve-year-old. Must be the alien tonic you're all drinking, eh?'

He grinned.

'Well, real pigs can't fly, but I did make all the Power Piglets in the world fly,' I said.

Dad laughed again.

'Oh, Sonny. You've really made my day with your comedy.'

'I'm not making it up, Dad. It's true. I *do* have superpowers and I saved the world from Auntie Cleo.'

'You saved the world from your aunt? I know she's a bit of a crook but she's hardly some big criminal mastermind.' He shook his head. 'I guess you've always had a very active imagination.'

'I know Mum hasn't told you yet, but Auntie Cleo wanted me to use my superpowers to steal all the money in the world. I didn't, of course, but I did get my own back by teleporting her and her boyfriend to the middle of a jungle.'

'Jungle? Teleporting? What on earth are you talking about, Sonny?' said Dad, rolling his eyes. 'I think you need to start cutting down on the number of comics you're reading. The next thing you'll be telling me is that you can fly like Superman.'

'Erm, actually I *can* fly.'

'OK, Sonny. Whatever you say. But this sounds like a load of nonsense to me,' said Dad.

So all I could do was prove to him that I had powers. I levitated up until I was hovering just beneath the ceiling.

Immediately Dad stared at me open-mouthed.

'Do you believe me now? And like I said, I can also teleport, and I can move things with my mind.'

Dad was completely flabbergasted.

'Fried onions!' he muttered. 'No, this has to be a dream.' He rubbed his eyes. 'I'm still in the coma, aren't I?'

'No, Dad, you're awake and this really is happening.'

I came back down and as my brain started to buzz, with my powers I lifted his beaker and made it move around us.

'How is the cup doing that? I must be seeing things. I have to be!' Dad insisted.

'It's me who's moving it, Dad, honestly,' I said, as I grabbed the beaker from the air. 'Look, I'll go and get Mum. She'll tell you I have powers.'

'Is it true, Bev? Does Sonny really have super-powers?' Dad asked Mum after she came in.

'Yes, Adam, it's true,' she replied, stroking my head.

'I told him about Auntie Cleo and Mick,' I said to her.

'So Sonny's told you how he saved the day by getting rid of my terrible sister and her awful boyfriend?' said Mum.

Dad nodded slowly.

'This is just so … incredible,' he muttered. 'Well, I never! I have a son who's a superhero!'

Hearing Dad say this made me feel super happy.

'I have always believed you were meant for greatness, but never did I imagine you'd be possibly greater than any human there has ever been!' Dad exclaimed.

'I've got lots more to tell you,' I said.

'Yeah, you mentioned something about flying Power Piglets. So what happened there?'

I smiled. 'It's probably best I start from the beginning.'

CHAPTER 53

The following weekend, I finally went to have my free ice cream at Ice To Meet You, and Delilah allowed me to have several scoops of three different flavours of my choice. I chose raspberry, chocolate fudge and my absolute favourite, cookie dough, which of course were all dairy-free.

I was very surprised to see Mr Goodwin in the ice-cream parlour, sitting alone in one of the booths.

'I thought you didn't like ice cream, sir,' I said to him.

'I don't, but as you can see, I thought I'd try out their waffles,' he said, pointing down at his plate.

'You should still try their ice creams, though. They're well yummy.'

But Mr Goodwin just wobbled his head, uninterested.

'You better enjoy that while you can,' said Delilah, sitting down on the chair opposite. Her face was glum.

'Why do say that?' I asked.

'I don't know how much longer we're going to be in business,' she whispered. 'The landlord wants to sell the whole building, including the ice-cream parlour, and there's a good chance the building could be demolished.'

'Oh no!' I said, aghast, wondering how I was going to live without my ice creams.

Delilah nodded sadly. 'I'm hoping it won't happen, because this place isn't just an ice-cream parlour, it's also our home. I love living above it. Now my parents are thinking about moving away, but I don't want to have to leave our school or Delmere.'

'Well, I'll keep my fingers crossed that none of that happens,' I said, holding up two crossed fingers. 'Because I'll really miss this place,' I added, *and I'll really miss you,* I said, but only in my head.

'Thanks,' Delilah replied, with a small smile, before getting up to clear a table in one of the booths.

I didn't feel like eating my ice cream after that. Hearing that the parlour might close, and that Delilah might move away, was truly the worst news.

Poor Delilah.

I watched as she sullenly wiped down the table in the booth and then knelt down to clean up slops of ice cream on the floor. I looked back at my ice cream as I joylessly put a spoonful in my mouth. Then I glanced back at Delilah, but she wasn't in the booth. It was like she'd totally vanished! I looked around to see if anyone else had noticed, but most people were too busy enjoying their ice creams and conversations to have paid any attention.

I went over to the booth, and I don't know why, but I looked under the table as though she were hiding there, but the only thing I could see was a spoon on the floor. My eyes searched the parlour again to see if Delilah was somewhere else, and when I spun back round, there she was, sitting in the booth.

'You were gone but … now you're back,' I muttered with shock.

'No, I was here the whole time,' she insisted, as her eyes looked around the parlour.

'No, you definitely vanished. The only thing that was here was a spoon.' I looked at the floor. 'It's gone. The spoon, it's not there!'

That's when it all clicked, and I looked at Delilah closely. 'You *do* have a superpower!' I whispered.

Delilah automatically shook her head, but then sighed and nodded. She looked around again.

'Not in here. Let's go outside and I'll tell you about it.'

I followed her out and we walked around the corner. I was feeling both stunned and thrilled that I'd finally met someone else with a superpower.

'I did wonder if you had a superpower after that evening when you disappeared and there was a teddy on the counter and then you appeared again, but then I thought, *Probably not*. I also thought Liam had a superpower because he'd got really good at the high jump, but that was only because his parents hired a private coach ...' My words came out in a rush.

Delilah threw me a puzzled look, then said, 'You knew about my superpower?'

I shrugged. 'I sort of guessed. So what type of power is it? Can you make yourself invisible?'

Delilah took a breath. 'Look, I will tell you, but only if you promise to keep it to yourself.'

'I will, I swear.'

Taking another breath, she said, 'I can shapeshift into literally anything, except people, for some reason. I don't know why. I also can't change into food, which I guess is a good thing, as I'd hate to be eaten.'

I blinked at her in astoundment.

'The thing is, my power has kind of got a few issues. Sometimes I just transform spontaneously when really I don't want to.' She tilted her head. 'That spoon on the floor was me, and the teddy bear that day? Well, that was me too.'

'You're a shapeshifter!' I gasped. Then my stomach lurched. 'You're not an alien, are you?'

'No, I'm not an alien,' said Delilah, sounding offended at such a question.

'Yeah, course, I know that,' I replied quickly, and breathed out a small sigh of relief. 'So what's it like being a shapeshifter?'

'Most of the time I don't even know what I'm going to turn into. But how it works is: if I've seen something and it stays in my memory, the next thing I know I'm a pigeon or a hat or a mirror. With the teddy bear, there was a little kid who had a bear that looked the same, and my body just went and replicated it.'

'It doesn't look like it lasts very long, though,' I remarked.

'Usually it doesn't, thank goodness. But there have been a few times when it's lasted *hours* and my parents haven't known where I am, not realising that the rug they're stepping on is actually me or that I'm the umbrella they're taking out in the rain.'

'Yikes! That doesn't sound great.'

'Tell me about it,' said Delilah.

'I've got a secret of my own too,' I began. 'You might

be surprised to know that you're not the only one with a superpower.'

It was now Delilah's turn to look amazed. 'You have a superpower as well?'

'Yeah, I can fly and teleport and move things with my mind. But please could you keep this a secret?'

'I will, I promise. Can I see your powers?' Delilah asked excitedly.

I looked around just to make sure no one was watching, then as my mind began to buzz, I made my phone float out of my jacket pocket and made it hover between me and Delilah.

'That's incredible!' she exclaimed as I grabbed my phone and put it back in my pocket. 'And you did that with your mind?'

'Yep.'

'So when did your powers start? Have you always had them?' asked Delilah.

'No, I've not had them for that long.'

'Me neither. I've only had this power for a few weeks,' said Delilah. 'Hey, do you think there might be other kids who have superpowers like us?'

'There could be. The abilities we have might be linked to something called the Delmere Magic, which is a phenomenon that has caused kids in this town to develop powers. It's been going on for centuries, apparently.'

'Wow, that's wild!' said Delilah, blinking rapidly.

Just then Mr Goodwin came round the corner, and as he walked past he was gazing at us curiously, which made my heart drum in my chest.

I swallowed. 'See you, Mr Goodwin.'

'Yes, bye,' he said, then quickly stumbled off.

Both Delilah and I shared a nervous look.

'You don't think he heard what we were saying, do you?' she whispered.

'I don't know,' I replied, but then I batted my hand dismissively. 'If he did, he's the type of person who wouldn't believe it anyway.' And even if he did happen to see what I did with my phone, he'd only think it was a magic trick or something,' I tried to reassure her.

And I just hoped I was right.

CHAPTER 54

A few days later, Dad was discharged from the hospital, and we threw him the welcome home party that we'd promised. We invited several of our neighbours, including Mrs Armstrong, Mr and Mrs Okaru and Blessing, Mr Donohue, Miss Lister and her son Gavin, Mrs Moretti and her family, and Mr Irvine and his family. It was so brilliant having Dad back home, and it was nice having our neighbours celebrate his return with us. As Dad was still on the mend, I was doing lots to help him out, such as using my powers to bring him the telephone or tea and biscuits – my way of making his life a little bit easier. Dad was still struggling to get his head around the fact that I had superpowers and would say, 'Baked bananas!' any time he'd see me using them.

My parents were stunned when I told them about the Delmere Magic. Like Mum, Dad had never heard of it either. Only, Dad wasn't as convinced as me that it was the source of my abilities. Instead, he decided that my superpowers were simply the result of a miracle. 'A blessing from the stars' he called it. But what was great was hearing him tell me again how proud of me he was.

Mum and Dad also let me babysit again when they went out to dinner one evening, and when they asked me, I was truly staggered, considering how badly my last effort at babysitting went. But Ramona and Oscar behaved very well. I think my warning them that I wouldn't take them flying if they wrecked the house could've had something to do with it. At school, my popularity continued much longer than I expected. But I think everyone in Year Seven was just thankful they could finally walk along the east entrance without getting cornered by Milo and his gang.

'So what's next in your superhero adventures?' asked Elliot as we walked to school one morning.

'And exactly what adventures are you talking about?' I asked him, intrigued.

'Well, I thought after ending Milo Allerton's reign of terror and saving the entire world from your greedy aunt and her boyfriend, you'd want to do something even more heroic.'

'Like what? Because I don't think it gets bigger than saving the world – unless I'd be required to save the galaxy.'

'Well, I think you could put your heroism to good use by telling Delilah how much you like her – and don't think I haven't noticed, because it's *so* obvious,' said Elliot, nudging me.

My cheeks suddenly grew warm.

'I just like her as a friend,' I muttered, lowering my eyes.

'Yeah, right,' said Elliot sarcastically.

I glanced back at him and sighed.

'*OK*. I do really like her,' I admitted, though the thought of telling Delilah about my feelings felt way harder than the prospect of having to save the galaxy. 'Do you think she can tell that I like her?'

Elliot shrugged. 'Dunno, but what I *do* know is that every good superhero needs a good sidekick. And even though I'd be of no use helping you battle an army of space aliens, I could always give you a few hints on what you could say to Delilah if you do fancy letting her know how smitten you are.'

He nudged me again.

'Well, if I do need any help with that, I'll let you know,' I said. 'Though, I wouldn't mind your help in thinking of a way I could really put my superpowers to good use again without everyone knowing that I have them. After the chaos with the Power Piglets and the earthquake I caused, *and* damaging my neighbours' roofs and cars, I feel like I've got quite a lot to make up for.'

'Didn't you say Ice To Meet You was being threatened with closure?'

I nodded.

'So you could start there. You could help save it!' said Elliot. 'And I'm sure most people in this town would be grateful, considering there are so many who seem to love that place.'

'Yeah! I could ask Delilah if she'd want to set up a campaign to save it, and I could offer to help her out.'

'Which would be a great way of getting to know her some more,' said Elliot, grinning. 'So as you can already see, I make a pretty good sidekick, don't you think?'

'Yeah, I think you'd be a cool sidekick!' I smiled.

Thinking back to when I first discovered I had superpowers, I could never have predicted all the things that went on to happen in my life. It's been an interesting journey so far, and although there have been some upsets, there have also been triumphs, like my dad being on the road to recovery and me not having to worry about

Milo Allerton. And seeing as I could now officially call myself a superhero, if Delmere, the world, or even the entire galaxy ever found itself in need of help, then I was ready to do whatever I could. I was ready to be … the STUPENDOUS SONNY!

ACKNOWLEDGEMENTS

I would like to give a huge thanks to my editor, Carla Hutchinson, and the team at Bloomsbury. Special thanks to my agent, Rachel Mann, for your continued support and guidance. Thank you to Chaaya Prabhat for your fantastic cover illustration, and thanks and love to my friends and family.

HAVE YOU READ

TURN THE PAGE
FOR A SNEAK PEEK ...

CHAPTER 1

Has something completely astounding and spectacular but also totally surprising ever happened to you? My name is Prune Melinda Robinson. I'm eleven years old, and something like that has just happened to me. Something so extraordinary, so out of this world, I'm still amazed by it now! And I bet you will be too.

I'll never forget the day my life changed forever ...

It all started one Sunday. It was a perfectly ordinary day, well, so I thought: I ate my lunch as usual and went back upstairs to my room. But then, as I went and sat down on my bed, I was suddenly surrounded by the most amazing colours all bunched together like clouds.

Magenta, coral, teal, lavender, and so many shades of yellow – the colour of sweet lemonade, sunflowers and cheese on toast – plus reds, which were redder than the tastiest strawberries and my mama's favourite lipstick. Not only that, but amongst the colour clouds were the greenest greens and the brownest browns, the pinkest pinks and blues the colour of lagoons, and not forgetting my favourite colour of all, orange, which shone as beautiful as a sunrise.

I pinched myself and rubbed my eyes to make sure I wasn't dreaming because it was as if I'd been transported to the most magnificent and enchanting place, my bedroom feeling like a forest of endless bloom. Though, when I reached out to touch the colours, I couldn't feel a thing.

The colours were all so bright – brighter than the sky and even brighter than the moon when it gets all big and fat and sits outside your window like it wants to move in.

They were even brighter than my grandpa's smile, and no one had a smile quite as bright as Poppa B. Well, no one except Grandma Jean. Her smile was more brilliant than the ruby earrings she liked to wear, a gift from Poppa after they got married. She wore them to his funeral – her earrings and her smile the only things that were cheerful on that bleak November day.

Some people didn't get why my grandma looked so happy when they were crying and wailing, even those that didn't know my poppa but had only turned up because they'd heard Mama was making her famous

4

potato salad for the wake. That's what my brother Jesse told me anyway.

But Grandma Jean said she had already cried all the tears she had when Poppa first got sick, and when the cancer began to make him weaker and smaller until it finally took away that beautiful bright smile of his. So when he died, Grandma made sure smiling was all she did because even though she was sad, most of all she was just grateful that Poppa wasn't suffering any more.

And now Grandma's gone too. She died two and a half months ago and I've been missing her heaps. Sometimes I get so sad that it feels like I have a shattered plate where my heart should be that no amount of superglue can put back together.

There was so much already that had changed in my life before the bizarre events of that day, and trying to get used to a world without Grandma had been the biggest change of all. To add to all this, I was about to start a new school the next day, *and* we'd just moved to a new house. Well, it was actually the house that had belonged to Grandma and Poppa B in a town called Delmere. A place where people say nothing interesting ever happens.

That was until that Sunday, when *everything* changed.

CHAPTER 2

'Prune!' my brother called from his bedroom, which is adjacent to mine. 'I've got a present for you. Prune!'

At the sound of his voice, the colours started to fade, shrinking like dots until there were just a few hanging above my head like a sparkly crown.

'What present?' I called back curiously, forgetting my worries about starting my new school the next morning and how strange it felt to be in this house without Grandma Jean.

'Come and take a look!' he said.

I went into Jesse's room to find him standing on his bed, replacing a picture of a meadow with a poster of his favourite basketball player, Titus Reid. He'd not long started unpacking his boxes, whereas I'd unpacked all my things when we moved in two days earlier. Although Jesse's room is bigger than mine, it most definitely isn't as nice. Everything is grey. Grey wallpaper, grey rug, grey curtains.

My room might be the smallest, but to me, it's the best room in the house. It used to be Grandma and Poppa's guest room, and it has these sweet little ornaments that include a set of dancing ballerinas and a lamp that's shaped like a tortoise. I could've put them in the cellar where we'd put most of Grandma Jean's things, but they were all so lovely I decided to keep them. Before we moved, Jesse and I used to share a room, so it was great to finally have a bedroom all to myself, especially as Jesse has a habit of farting *a lot*.

A long time ago, Jesse's room belonged to Mama. On the wall, it still has the tiny marks she drew to track her height when she was a young girl. The lines only go up a little way because Mama is quite short. I am already nearly as tall as her, and she thinks I'll soon grow past her just like Jesse has. He's fifteen and is close to six feet, but I'd never want to grow that tall. I'd just like to be medium-sized – a height that's halfway between Mama and Jesse.

'Here's your present,' said Jesse, handing me the picture of the meadow. 'I was going to put it with Grandma's stuff, but then I thought you might like it.'

'Thanks.' I smiled, taking a closer look at the picture.

It was actually quite pretty and had been painted

with watercolours. I knew this because art is one of my favourite things in the whole world, and you'll never catch me without my sketchbook. I love drawing just as much as I love superhero films, mint-scented bath bombs, red velvet cupcakes, chocolate ice cream and my butterfly hair clips that look like real butterflies.

I'm actually an award-winning artist, having come second place at my old school's annual art competition a few months back. It was for my picture of a dolphin doing an aerial somersault. Plus I came third in a big inter-school competition with my picture of Spider-Man web-swinging through New York City. My favourite picture ever is a portrait I did of Grandma, even though I didn't win an award for it. I was only seven when I drew it, and my drawing has improved a lot since then, but I still feel so proud because I know how much Grandma loved it.

It still amazes me how I got her to sit still for a whole hour and she didn't fidget once; not like Jesse when I tried to do his portrait. He could barely sit still for two minutes, let alone an hour. Hopefully, when I grow up and become a famous artist, I'll get to draw lots of people's portraits, including my favourite singer, Keirra Grace.

As I looked at the painting Jesse gave me, I knew I still had a long way to go before my pictures would be anywhere near as good. I'd love to live near a meadow. As far as I know, there aren't any meadows in Delmere, and there certainly weren't any meadows where we used to live – a neighbouring town called Ocean View. But it didn't exactly have an ocean either, or a lake or a river, and the only views I ever got were of the bins at the back of our old tower block. We did have Shellwood Park though, which had a basketball court and a playground, only Mama didn't like us going there because some local boys, or 'hooligans' as she preferred to call them, saw the park as theirs. Sometimes they'd even try and charge people to go in. One boy wanted Mama to pay him a pound when we went to have a picnic there one Saturday.

Mama told him, 'I don't know what you think you're doing, but you need to get out of my way right now, young man. And if you think you're getting a single penny out of me, you can think again!'

She tried to push open the gate, but the boy pushed it back, stopping us from going in. So, in the end, we had our picnic at home on the living room carpet.

'At least when we move, I won't have to keep fretting about you hanging around those hooligans,' Mama said to Jesse while we ate. 'And nor will I have to worry that you'll end up in some young offenders institution,' she added.

But Jesse just laughed and told Mama that she was overreacting.

'My friends aren't hooligans, Mama. And why worry? Nothing bad is going to happen to me.'

But his response made Mama extra cross.

'I worry because you're my son, Jesse,' she said, her voice as firm as it gets. 'And I'll never stop worrying, even when you're a man in his fifties, and please stop laughing because none of this is funny.'

But that's just my brother. He never takes things seriously and thinks he's so smart when he still can't even solve my Rubik's cube. I've been solving it since I was eight! But there are some things Jesse's good at. He makes the most brilliant strawberry milkshakes and I suppose he's not half bad at telling a funny joke or two. Yet the problem with Jesse is that he just can't seem to understand that it's not smart to bunk off school, which he's done *a lot*.

You'd think he'd also know that if you're going to steal something from a shop, you'd better be prepared to get caught. But no, not Jesse. Not even after he got caught red-handed trying to steal chocolate from Thorne's Express. That's when I decided my brother must have his brain missing – why else would he be so stupid?

It wasn't the first time Jesse had stolen something either. He was really lucky the shop's owner, Mr Thorne, didn't call the police. But he did call Mama, who was furious, and it was only when she threatened to call the police on Jesse herself that my brother admitted that his friend Bryce had dared him to do it.

'So if Bryce Mackenzie dared you to jump off a bridge, would you do that too?' asked Mama when he returned home.

But Jesse just kept his head bowed, saying nothing.

'That's why Bryce and the rest of those *so-called friends* of yours aren't really your friends at all – not when they're busy trying to get you into trouble,' said Mama. 'And that had better be the last time I hear you've stolen something. You've got me feeling so ashamed, Jesse!'

Then she started to cry and I stared at Jesse long and hard as I hated seeing Mama cry.

But as I looked at him across the living room, I wondered if he had a heart missing too, because it was like he just didn't care. Not one bit.

'Stop staring, Pugface!' He scowled at me.

Pugface is a name Jesse calls me when he wants to be horrible. But it's only because he knows his name isn't as sweet as mine.

'But why would anyone want a dozy name like *Prune*?' he once said when I told him he was jealous. 'And Mama's just as dozy naming you after some ugly bugly fruit that makes people want to do number twos!'

Not that Jesse would dare say that to Mama's face. But anyway, I don't care what he thinks of my name because I love it, hugely. Plus I happen to think prunes are super delicious.

Jesse's been friends with Bryce since he was eleven, ever since Bryce beat up a boy who was picking on him. After that he became my brother's hero, replacing Poppa B, who'd been a hero to us both. Bryce used to go to Jesse's old school – well, that was until he got permanently excluded for constantly bunking off. But for some reason, Jesse still looks up to Bryce, or at least acts as though he owes him something. I reckon it's because he thinks Bryce is somehow living some ultra-cool life just because he's seventeen and has his own car and got his dad to convert their garage into a gym. His family have lots of money, but Bryce likes to steal and walks around acting like he's as hard as Iron Man. I only wish Jesse could see that Bryce isn't someone worth getting into trouble for.

'Earth to Prune, hello!' Jesse droned through a rolled-up poster, snapping me out of my thoughts. 'You've got the picture, so you can go now.'

'Jesse, can you see these colours?' I said, pointing above my head where the dots had been.

'Huh? What colours?'

I looked up and then went over to his mirror to double-check. The colours had now completely vanished. But just where had they come from? Or had it simply been my eyes playing tricks on me?

ABOUT THE AUTHOR

Ellie Clements was born in London and decided she wanted to become an author at the age of nine, when her favourite hobby was writing short stories. Her passion for writing continued and she later studied journalism at university. Ellie's working life has mostly been spent in the charity sector, and when she isn't busy writing for children, she enjoys long walks, browsing her local bookshop and the occasional spot of karaoke.